Liberty or Death

Death

by David Cook

LIBERTY OR DEATH

is dedicated to the people of Northern Ireland and the Republic of Ireland

Horror came to *Uaimh Tyrell*.

It was a poor village, as it had been in Tudor times, and had never expanded like neighbouring Blackwater or Skreen. Richard Tyrell had been a *buanadha,* an Irish mercenary, who had fought for Hugh O'Neill during the Nine Years War against Queen Elizabeth's English troops. It was Tyrell that led Spanish mercenaries sent from Phillip II to assist the Irish uprising en-route to Ulster, and the meeting place was in one of the dark coastal caves that gave the village its name.

It lay along the east coast of Wexford about six miles north of the town bearing the same name as the county. A small stream named *Banna*, meaning 'goddess', flowed out to sea through a gully to a shingle beach where fishing boats worked the deep waves. The rest of the villagers herded sheep on the hills and farmed the land. *Uaimh Tyrell* was a collection of thatched huts huddled around a small stone church where Father Ciarán prayed to the bones of Saint Brigid. The Saint had visited the original village church before founding the great abbey at Kildare sometime in the fifth century. The converted church in her name was given the sacred bones when she was exhumed in order to prevent Viking invaders plundering them from the convent many years later. Her head was taken to Lisbon, her remains were scattered, and the four bones that kept in the hamlet's church were from her hands.

'They're not the bones from her hands,' Lochlann the Elder would say to anyone that enquired. 'Father Ciarán is a pious soul, but the man's mad! Utterly mad! They're the bones from a red fox! By the love of God, he prays to a fox!'

The bones were small, thin and ochre-brown in colour, and could have come from a red deer, or indeed a fox, but the elderly Father Ciarán would have none of it. He made his daily prayers to them underneath a Saint Brigid's cross, a cross-shaped symbol made from tied rushes containing a woven square in the centre and tied off ends. The children of the village had made this one for the Saint's day, and Ciarán proudly hung it above the open box containing her consecrated bones.

The sacred village was a place of worship, fish, cattle, rain and wind-swept hills. Where dreams were wished for and prayers rarely answered.

And on this day the redcoats came.

The first thing Ciarán heard was the sound of the cockerels crowing loudly in alarm, horses hooves thumping the ground like distant peals of thunder, growing instead of dying, and young Dónall's dog barking madly. Then there were screams that split the morning air; sounds that chilled his heart. His pulse quickened. He opened the church door and instantly a pair of scarred hands shoved him violently back inside the nave.

'Get back, you bible-humping turd!' a man spat at him, a great drip of spittle fell from thick lips to glisten on his coat. 'Back with you!'

Father Ciarán tripped on his cassock and landed on the hard stone floor. Three men, dressed in the red coat of the military, stepped over him; steel spurs jingled with each step. Their looming shadows reached the far wall to touch the altar.

'Please,' the priest begged, 'this is a house of God.'

'Better start reciting your prayers then, you piece of filth,' said the thick-lipped one, giving a lupine grin. He had immense shoulders, and powerfully-built arms and legs.

Manic prickles raced across Ciarán's skin. 'Why have you come here? What do you want?'

None of them answered. Next to the muscular one, the other two looked of the same mould; rough of face and of a similar age. They were cavalrymen who wore topped black leather boots, white breeches, black bicorn hats with a tall black plume and their single-breasted red jackets were faced black. Ciarán had not seen these men before, but they were fellow Irishmen and served the Crown. They also carried carbines, which were still hooked to their white shoulder belts with a clip, but it was the long straight-bladed swords that gave them the fearsome edge to their appearance.

These men were killers.

Outside, the villagers were being brought out of their homes by dismounted troopers. More horsemen, maybe thirty, were encircling the village. One man tried to resist and was punched to the ground. A woman howled, bright blood streamed down her face, as she was brought outside.

Long legs climbed the few stone steps of the church and a figure blocked the doorway. The silver-haired priest had to shield his rheumy eyes from the low sun in order to see the newcomer's face. A glint of gold buttons and a crimson sash revealed that he was an officer.

'I knew of a leper that once lived in this village,' the silhouetted man said in a clear and precise voice. He took off one of his long white gloves and slapped the front of his immaculate scarlet coat with it to dislodge invisible lint.

One of the two similar troopers took a step back. 'A leper, sir?' he swallowed hard.

All men fear the grey and rotting gnarled flesh of lepers. Most were treated in hospitals, but some were sent out into the wilds to live as they must, begging for food and clothing, hoping for salvation.

Father Ciarán nodded. 'Gerrit used to live up on the bluff. But he died five winters past.'

'What the hell was a bloody lazar doing here?' the trooper seemed to tremble. He scratched his white powdered hair at the neckline. In this heat, the men, except the officer who did not seem to follow procedure, found their hair itchy from the lice, grime and sweat.

'Gerrit wanted solitude and found it here,' Ciarán replied. 'He was a gentle soul and a good man.'

'And the kind and charitable Father Ciarán looked after him?' the officer said with a touch of sarcasm. 'Isn't that correct?'

Ciarán stiffened. 'I did. It is my duty to help the sick, the needy and the poor. We are all God's children.'

The officer snorted through his long canted nose. 'I understand that you look after all of your people. Isn't that true?'

Ciarán didn't reply, he swung his craggy gaze up at the man who took a step forward into view. He had raven black hair, a thin mouth and piercingly cold eyes.

'Where is the blacksmith?'

Ciarán guessed there would be no appeasing the man, for he looked bitter and sinful, yet he had to protect his people. 'I don't know.'

The chill eyes matched the officer's expression. 'I want the truth.'

The priest remained mute. He could hear shouting and sobbing, and he made the sign of the cross on his chest.

The officer signalled with a dip of his head and immediately the muscular trooper kicked Ciarán in the ribs, hard enough to fracture bone. Ciarán was propelled along the stones by the force of the vicious attack. He lay clutching his thin chest, gasping and wincing in pain.

The officer smiled. 'I've seen Seamus kick a man to death, Father. It didn't take him long, but every second for the victim was agony. So I'll ask you one more time.' He was calm, almost chillingly composed, as he moved into the church, spurs jangling with every step. 'Where is the blacksmith? I know he's called Scurlock. Where's his boy? Dónall, isn't it? Sable hair, freckles and he's got a scar underneath an eye from an accident with a hoe. Where are they?'

Father Ciarán gaped at the officer's knowledge. 'Please, sir,' he pleaded, making a mewing sound as the officer then ordered the thatch-roofed smithy to be torched. He reached forward to grab the tall officer's thigh, but Seamus stamped his boot on Ciarán's back and then kicked him in the face, dislodging a front tooth.

'I don't think he knows where this fellow Scurlock is, sir,' said one of the two troopers, staring at the blood streaming through the old man's fingers.

The officer swivelled resentful eyes on the man, who could not keep his gaze and, instead, looked down and fingered his carbine's trigger.

'Nonsense,' the officer said dismissively, 'we all know the people trust and confide in their priests. They are the ears, eyes and mouths of the rebels. They are the scourge of the land. They are the source of this insurrection. Breathing it, preaching it. They fan the fires with their sermons. They serve the Cause first and God second.' He turned to Seamus. 'If he won't talk, cut off his ears; then cut out his eyes and if he still remains silent, cut out his tongue. You may then do as you will.' He gave the priest a look of revulsion. 'Let's see if the rebels miss one of their own.' He turned away to walk outside.

Ciarán stirred. 'Please,' he said, his voice barely a whisper and thick with blood, 'we have nothing to do with the unrest. Scurlock is a good man. I've known him since he was a boy. He'd never hurt a soul, or get himself tangled up in the insurrection.'

The officer stopped to turn around and face him. 'He's a blacksmith, and the smiths are the weapon makers for the devious traitors. I want to question him in connection with the murder of two of my men.' His face was a rictus of anger and sharp teeth. 'For the last time, where is he?'

The old man trembled, eyes glinting with tears. 'Have mercy!'

There would be none.

The officer stepped away and the last thing Father Ciarán saw was Seamus lean over him, and the wicked knife went to work. The peacefulness of village life suddenly became one of unimaginable torment.

The village was filled with more screams, for most of the women and children were still alive and their ordeal had scarcely begun. All the young women were saved from immediate slaughter, because they were raped first. The older ones were herded with the men and cut down. One auburn-haired woman was crying, not because a man with yellow teeth and rancid breath had dragged her near the *Banna* by her hair, but because her two boys were still inside her home that was flickering with flame and smoke. The man had lifted her skirts and was on top, rutting like a wild hog, impervious to her tear-stained pleas.

A few shots rang out from carbines as one or two men tried to fight back, but the bullets killed them. A man rolled on the ground and two horsemen leant down from their saddles, taking it in turns to slash his body with their swords. Another, dressed in a white shirt and tan knee-breeches, managed to break free and scramble up the road towards Blackwater, but a pistol banged from the church steps to send him flying in a spray of crimson. The body twitched. Blood trickled obscenely over the stones.

An officer, mounted on a ghost-grey horse, trotted over to the church as a piercing scream echoed from within. He wiped his forehead with a handkerchief and looked down to the tall dark officer. "Tis a fine pistol, sir,' Captain McGifford said appreciatively.

Colonel Black glanced at the weapon. It was rifled with highly decorative hunting scenes in silver mounts running along the walnut stock to the barrel. It was an exquisite piece of craftsmanship, and one he highly treasured. His servant, a trooper, held onto his horses reins.

'The quicker they fall, the easier the end shall be,' he said smiling, which was as welcoming as a blizzard.

'I do hope that wasn't our man Scurlock, sir?'

Black's lips tightened in anger. 'Then I wouldn't have fired my piece, Captain,' he said, giving the officer a venomous glare. 'Do you take me for an imbecile?'

'No, sir.' McGifford coughed to cover his embarrassment at the rebuke. 'None of the villagers knew where the blacksmith and his boy have gone.'

Black stared up to where the stream fell gently over dark rocks and thick grass covered in marsh thistle. He could see a pair of white legs and the auburn-haired woman appeared to be wearing a necklace of red gemstones.

'That one revealed earlier that Scurlock has a brother in New Ross, so that's where we'll go next.'

'I see, sir. She was pretty wee thing,' McGifford commented on the dead woman with the slashed throat. 'A shame that.'

'Careful McGifford,' Black warned, lifting his gaze. 'One must remember that they plot to overthrow our government and murder our people. I'll not have a man under my command think otherwise. We have those that were close to us to avenge in this bloody affair.'

'Yes, sir,' McGifford spoke ruefully. 'Of course, sir. I was only talking about her beauty.'

Black watched as two draft horses and one fine horse that could serve as a trooper's spare mount, as well as silver from the church, was being collected by his exultant men and packed into a covered wagon. He was pleased with their work today. No losses to the ranks. Another victory, so easily achieved. A pity the smith wasn't apprehended, but no matter. Time was running out for the man.

They left behind a smouldering, stinking ruin. Bodies lay in heaps, cherry-red embers glowed and seagulls circled high over *Uaimh Tyrell* like carrion birds.

The horsemen rode south.

*

It was a week later.

Fists pounded down on the desk, ink spilled, and cream-coloured papers swept down onto the polished marbled floor.

'The whole village was destroyed!' said a voice that made the half-dozen officers in the room all jump at once. The man who spoke was a tall Scotsman called John Moore. 'The people were massacred! Butchered into offal! Is this what this wretched conflict has become? A slaughter yard?' he asked and no one answered him. 'Is this the work of Colonel Black?'

'It appears so, sir,' replied an aide, braving Moore's unusual temper that flared sudden like black powder in the priming pan.

'It could well be the work of the rebels, sir,' suggested another. 'Trying to incite more unrest?'

Colonel Moore gave his opinion of the matter in the shortest terms. He stared out one of the windows of Dublin Castle, the thick-walled seat of British rule, where sentries, bayonet-tipped muskets and polished cannons guarded it from enemies. There was a curfew, still in effect after rebels planned to storm the Castle a fortnight ago, but the men were ill-led and had no cohesion, so the attack had failed. However, the threats of other attacks were still on everyone's mind, so only servicemen and state officials could be allowed out after dark and all had to have signed papers. He sighed to expel the temper raging hot inside him like a forge's fire.

'While we try and instil a sense of diplomacy and stability to the people of this land,' he remarked, turning to the men, 'we allow men like Colonel Black to haunt the thoroughfares in order to murder and butcher at will,' Moore continued, glancing down at the table where a list of atrocities were said to have been committed by this particular man. 'I am utterly appalled.'

"Colonel Black" was just a name coined by the press for the unknown, shadowy figure that roamed the highways inflicting torture and death in the name of the king. The government had put a price on his head at a thousand guineas, but he remained at large, and no one who had seen his face had lived to tell the tale. Religion has played no part in this. Black was a malevolent spectre; a bogeyman that preyed on the rich and poor, and so far his crusade of blood and terror had hindered any peaceful resolution between the government and the insurgents.

Moore gave a weary sigh and rubbed his temples with his fingertips. It was a swelteringly humid night and he undid the buttons on his white waistcoat to let it fall open and reveal a white silk shirt underneath. The back of it was soaked with sweat. 'Bring me Mullone,' he asked exasperatedly. 'Send in the major now.'

The aides shuffled out and a moment later the wide doors opened and a blond officer was seen into the room. The twin doors closed silently behind him. Lorn Mullone was dressed in a uniform style based on the British Light Dragoons; his scarlet coat had green facings, the colour of spring grass, and buff breeches, which on closer inspection were stained and worn with age. His Tarleton helmet with its white over red plume and black crest was battered and tucked under an arm.

'Have a seat, Lorn,' Moore gestured hospitably to one of the chairs.

'Thank you, sir,' Mullone's voice was soft and warm. He was a slim built man, with a wide-jawed freckled face. His green eyes revealed intelligence, warmth and trust. He shook Moore's proffered hand.

'How was your journey? Not too troublesome, I hope?'

'Not at all, sir.'

'You have your reports?'

'I do,' Mullone had brought with him several detailed reports of his findings; firsthand accounts, Militia and Yeomanry information, rebel dispositions and eye-witness descriptions. He read them all to Moore who appeared tense throughout the reading.

Tea, bread, butter, ham and cold chicken were brought to the room, mainly for the major who was tired and famished, having spent the last two days in the saddle riding down from Ulster.

'You may remove your coat, neck-tie and undo your waistcoat like I, Lorn,' Moore gestured with a ghost of a smile. 'It's devilishly muggy.'

'Thank you kindly, sir,' Mullone said, his hair at his temples and back of his neck were darkened with sweat. He undid the buttons on his scarlet coat, revealing a red-collared waistcoat underneath decorated in silver lace and buttons. He loosened the white silk neck-tie and dropped it into a pocket. He placed the helmet on the floor and draped his fraying coat over the back of the chair as no aides were present to take them.

Moore waited until Mullone had finished his supper. 'Colonel Black and his marauders have been terrorising the people of Wicklow and Wexford, and so far have not been apprehended. In fact, he has eluded every arresting party sent to find him. He's one step ahead every time.'

'How so, sir?'

Moore scratched his chiselled face. 'I really don't know how he does it. Damned good luck?' He shot Mullone a stale look. 'It has been reported that Black is English and his men are English Dragoon Guards, but that is a source of speculation having been solely reported in the press. It also seems there are conflicting rumours on his namesake. Some will tell you it's because he rides a black horse, some say it's because the troop he commands have black facings, while others will claim it's because his heart is as black as the Devil. I even heard one of the Castles' guards say that storm clouds herald his attacks.' He scornfully shook his head. 'Preposterous! He's just a man! Yet, his name is whispered in fear and the people are cowering whenever it is mentioned. He's a damned canker that needs cutting out. Peace will not come until the day he's stopped.'

Mullone dipped his head with agreement. 'Do we know what his motives are?'

'Apart from slaughter?' Moore said, lifting a wry eyebrow. 'Nothing that I'm aware of. There's nothing that points to his intentions, so we've not been able to second-guess him. He makes no demands.'

Mullone took a sip of tea, savouring the taste. 'When did the first atrocity occur?'

'Three weeks ago a Militia captain from one of the garrison towns at the foot of the Wicklow Mountains is said to have allowed Colonel Black to release six prisoners from the gaol. Black and his men then hunted the felons down like foxes. The prisoners were apparently all arrested before the unrests had started and were not, as the captain testified at his court martial, conspirators or United men. It was cold-blooded murder and nothing more. And it seems Black has a taste for the sport.' A clock in the room struck twelve and Moore paused until the chiming stopped. 'Do you know of Torrington?'

Mullone's brow twitched a touch. 'Captain Ennis Torrington?'

'Yes, the very same. A contemptible fellow. He's now of the North Wicklow County Militia Regiment, and recently went on a bloody rampage with Black that, according to Sir Edward Clanfield, a local Wexford landowner, yielded five hundred pikes and thirty muskets taken from the rebels. Sir Edward's chilling account confirms that at least fifty were killed. I deduce that they were all rounded up and shot, or cut down where they stood. There are no indications that any of them were rebels, though. Torrington insists otherwise.' Moore sighed, as though he found what he was about to say disturbing. 'But it was last week that Black's savagery has caused this country new grief. It was a place called ⁻ '

'*Uaimh Tyrell*, sir,' Mullone interposed, knowing what the colonel was about to say. 'It's all I've heard about in the last two days. I can't quite believe it. It's despicable, so it is.'

Moore sighed heavily and stared into Mullone's pensive eyes. 'It was a hallowed place and he just butchered those poor people.'

'I know, sir,' Mullone said, voice tinged with sorrow.

'The village was a mix of Catholics and Protestants and he murdered them all. The women were abused in the most grotesque manner. The priest was found mutilated beyond all recognition.' Moore paused momentarily because it genuinely upset him. 'We don't know why he went there. In the weeks since the new insurgencies started, Black's attacks have worsened. A Wexford barrister was found hanging from a tree yesterday morning. Disembowelled and his eyes gouged out.'

An image of a young man with a rope tied around his neck instantly shot into Mullone's thoughts as Moore carried on talking. A cold wind blew. Snowflakes twirled and danced in the air. He could hear the creaking of the rope as the man slowly rotated to face him. He was dead. That was obvious. His neck was horribly distorted, face bloodless, eyes bulging and tongue exposed through purple lips. Mullone shivered at the image. It wasn't the first time; it usually came to him when he was dreaming.

'Lorn?' Moore asked, seeing his expression.

Mullone blinked and shook his head. 'I'm sorry, sir.' He paused, trying his best to get the image out of his mind. 'Please continue.'

'Apparently, Black is supposed to have been responsible. If you ask me, I think the rebels did it. The barrister was a loyalist and unfortunately, out of favour. The same goes for that magistrate that was shot by his own gamekeeper. It's not the first time the rebels have killed in revenge. And I'm afraid it won't be the last. But Black, in my opinion, was responsible for *Uaimh Tyrell.*'

'Is he a government man, sir?' Mullone asked.

'No,' Moore said vehemently.

'Is he English?'

'I suspect he's Irish gentry, but the rumour is that he commands English Dragoon Guards, which is nonsense. His men are said to wear red coats, but there's no mounted regiment that I know of with black facings.'

'Yeomanry? Fencible?'

'Nothing in the records,' Moore said.

The government had raised and equipped numerous Yeomanry corps of both horse and foot, but these were smaller formations than Militia, and usually confined to their own territories for garrison and patrol duties. The Fencible regiments were raised in defence against the threat of invasion in order to free up the regular Foot battalions fighting abroad.

Mullone grunted. 'Yet, Black dresses in the scarlet coat of an officer in King George's army.'

Moore thought he heard an accusation in the Irishman's tone and looked at his face for any signs of insolence, but there were none.

'I don't even know if he holds a colonel's rank,' Moore said. 'I suspect it's self-styled. The press have started to call him 'The King's Wrath', or 'Cromwell's Ghost', but they easily forget that Black murders anyone, regardless of their convictions. I want him caught before he strikes again. Earl Camden is putting pressure on me to bring him in. We can't have peace while he still operates. I want you to find out who he is, and stop him.'

Mullone sat upright. 'Sir?'

'I know you're tired, Lorn,' Moore said compassionately. 'God knows we all are, but I need your help. I don't have anyone else I can ask that I trust. You come highly recommended by Castlereagh. Camden has given me the powers in order to hunt Black's irregulars down. I've had some difficulty already from command. You've heard that Sir Ralph has stepped down?'

Mullone was surprised. 'No,' he gasped.

Sir Ralph Abercromby, Commander-in-Chief of the British Army, was regarded as an extremely compassionate man. His plan was to disarm the populace as quickly as possible by sending troops to live in those districts that were still actively rebellious. The aim was to frighten the people into handing over any weapons and to nullify them. It had worked hitherto in Kildare and Kilkenny, but General Lake was a ham-fisted, tactless individual, who had taken the reins of command with his usual unsympathetic aplomb, discarding Abercromby's plans of empathy for brutality.

'Sir Ralph resigned due to clashes with the Whigs. Parliament wasn't happy with his views on the gentry being "troublesome", and so rather than face any more opposition, which have deluged the press of late, he simply quit. General Lake is now in command,' Moore said it as though it was a warning. 'The Irish populace is treated worse than the slaves of Saint Lucia,' he said bitterly, knowing as the once succeeding Governor of the Caribbean island, how appalling behaviour can quickly instil resentment. 'It's not in my nature to criticise a senior officer, but his methods are purely barbaric. How can we win the people's affections when we're treating them like war criminals?'

'I agree, sir. You can't.'

'But you are a sympathetic man and a damned fine officer. Empathy will win this war, not bigotry and obstinacy. Do you have your men with you?'

'Yes, sir.'

It was a delicate question to ask, but Moore asked it anyway. 'Do you trust them?'

'Of course, sir.'

Moore gave a brief smile. 'You've certainly earned their trust.'

Mullone was a major in Lord Maxwell Lovell's Irish Dragoons. The regiment was only two years old, having been raised by Lord Lovell, a member of the Whig party, and who was currently in London. It was once a hundred men strong, but now Mullone commanded less than forty. When he had arrived to begin his duties as major, he discovered that the men were extremely lax and uncaring. Desertion was ripe. He considered himself a fair man and a good officer and immediately investigated as to why the men were so unhappy. It became apparent that Colonel Pennyfather was skimming money from the regiments pay chest, so in an eye-blink, Mullone had him arrested and the men immediately paid all back payments. They had cheered him like a king, and from that day he had earned their trust.

'And if you're wondering about your appointment,' Moore saw the slightest hesitation in the depths of Mullone's eyes, 'it was your reports that alerted the government to Bantry Bay.'

Mullone was currently employed by the War Office to spy on Theobald Wolf Tone, a protestant lawyer, and his acquaintance of a

French agent called De Marin. In Jersey, Mullone had intercepted a despatch from Tone to De Marin who was hiding somewhere in Cork. The codes revealed that thousands of men waited in flat-bottomed barges and troop ships. Mullone had quickly alerted the government to the French armada which left Holland for Ireland, and the army managed to repel the French landing at Bantry Bay, a small village on the south coast of Cork, during the bitterly cold winter of '96.

'Thank you, sir.'

'And if I'm not mistaken, the French calamity at Fishguard?'

Mullone smiled self-deprecatingly. 'I played a minor role, sir.'

A smaller French invasion fleet had stormed the Pembrokeshire coast in February '97, to which Mullone had managed to help defeat with the aid of local forces.

'Nonsense, I don't believe that for a moment. I have the utmost trust in your skills to find Black. You've got a natural talent for rooting out troublemakers. You've guile, tenacity and instinct. If anyone can find this black-hearted devil, then it's you.'

'Thank you for your kind estimation, sir.'

'Good. In the morning, I want you to take your men and head to New Ross. It's a town on the Kilkenny border, about forty miles west of Wexford.'

'Why New Ross, sir?' Mullone said cautiously, still thinking that he wasn't the right man for the job.

'I've received a letter from Colonel Robert Craufurd, who is the garrison commander of the town. Do you know the colonel?'

'I know of him, sir,' Mullone replied prudently. Bob Craufurd was said to be a difficult man and a strict disciplinarian, but a fine soldier nonetheless.

'He writes of a strange troop of cavalry outside the town. When they are questioned, they claim to be on an important mission from the government. There is no such standing. I've told him you're on your way.'

'Sounds rather odd, sir,' Mullone said suspiciously. 'Can we be clear on the matter of *modus operandi* if these fellows turn out to be Black and his irregulars?' Moore looked into the Irishman's eyes. 'Black and his men must be stopped. At all costs,' he rapped the table with his fingers. 'But he is to be apprehended alive! I want him to face a public trial. He must be made accountable for his crimes and punished in a court of law. The people need to see him brought to justice.'

'I understand.'

'God be with you, Lorn.'

'I hope He is, sir.' Mullone drank the last dregs of his tea before shaking hands with Moore and departing the room.

To hunt a killer for the sake of Ireland's future.

*

The first light of a new day blazed bright over County Wexford for a few seconds, lancing through the thin clouds like a glittering explosion.

A dawn mist hung between trees. Bark glistened. The air was already sticky, hazy and sparkled in the pooling mist that seemed to have washed away the stain and dust of the previous day. And yet, despite the dampness, it promised to be another beautiful summer's day in an otherwise wicked world.

And then the horsemen came.

They came out of the mist like creatures from a nightmare. They were dressed in the red finery of British Dragoon Guards, and the big horses thundered down the green tangle of sunken lanes with reckless abandonment. There were fifty of them, faces grim underneath black bicorn hats, and they cantered fast in pursuit of their prey.

The prey was in fact a man, who unknown to the troopers, had already negotiated his horse up the steep banks of the lane to lie concealed in the undergrowth's wild chaos. He watched them pass in a blur of horse, uniform and dust, waiting a few minutes until he was satisfied that he was safe, and then gently eased his horse up.

'There, there,' he said soothingly, patting its neck where the thick veins throbbed beneath the skin with large blackened calloused hands. He was a big man with broad shoulders, and a flat, hard face. The horse whinnied and jerked its head with fondness at his gentle touch.

He looked around. The patch of ground was covered in ferns and wood horsetails, skirted by ancient-looking trees with gnarly boughs. A red deer watched his movements, ears pricked, before bolting away. Hearing a soft trickle of water, he carefully negotiated up towards the high ground, feet snapping on old twigs and making a dull sound as his thighs brushed against the verdure. He reached the small bubbling stream, half-hidden by the ferns, and bent down to take a long drink. It was good and he cupped some for his horse. A blackbird sang its beautiful birdsong and a robin redbreast joined in; its call was louder despite its small stature. He pulled out a handful of corn from his long grey coat, and the horse munched noisily with big yellow teeth.

The man wiped sweat from his forehead when the corn was all gone, leaving husks on his skin, and yanked out a scrap of paper, which had an address on it. A slit of sunlight from the green canopy above dappled the clearing. He had risked his life to get this far, but the leader of the cavalry was a methodical and persistent bastard. One slip up, and the man knew he would be in loyalist hands and it would all be over. He had the address of a man who would help him, and now he just had to survive long enough to reach it.

Scurlock put the paper back in his pocket and followed the path through the woods to the town of New Ross where his brother, Pádraig and his son, Dónall would be waiting for him.

*

'Where exactly are we heading to, sir?' Sergeant Seán Cahill asked, before spitting a thick jet of chewing tobacco onto the roadside. His white breeches were spotted with spittle stains.

Mullone steered his horse around a charred shell of what appeared to have once been a mail coach. The rebels intercepted mail coaches and set them ablaze as a signal on the roads for the men to snatch up their pikes and green cockades, and meet at dedicated rendezvous points. The air was still and the horse's hooves kicked up dust, so the men and their mounts were grimy and dusty.

'New Ross, Seán,' he said, pulling at his neck-tie that seemed to choke him. 'We're to find this man, Colonel Black, and bring him back to the Castle.'

'Ah, that'll be nice,' Sergeant Cahill replied in his customary unbothered way. As usual Mullone was struck by the sergeant's ability to take everything in his stride, as though their hunt for a shadowy killer was just another adventure.

It was just after nine o'clock and the twenty-five-mile journey from Dublin had taken them three hours. They would have to rest properly soon, for the sake of their horses; having rode on and off for two days straight. Besides, the men were sore with chafed thighs and numb arses.

It was a beautiful June day. The sky was a brilliant corn-flower blue, speared by a dazzling and glittering sun. It had been the hottest May on record; certainly no one could remember a May that blisteringly hot, and now June too burned like an open kiln.

The dragoons made their way to the town across verdant fields and skirted great swathes of dark woodland. They discovered a moss-fringed stream where Mullone let the men fill their canteens and allowed the snorting horses a thirst-quenching drink before setting off again.

Tack and weaponry jangled and clinked and hoof beats thudded; those sounds were the only interruptions to the silence across the hazy fields.

Mullone gazed at the hedgerows, bright with flowers that edged along the wheel-rutted and hoof-churned road. A hare hopped onto the roadside a few yards away from the horsemen, then quickly disappeared back into tall grasses that were thick with catchfly, monkshood and corn cockle. Past the hedges, the warm morning sun seemed to hug the gentle fields. *Tintreach*, his grey stallion named Lightning in Gaelic, loped steadily, and he whispered soothing words into the beast's tall pricked ears. *Tintreach*, named because of the white lines that resembled sparks shooting from his hocks, was a sturdy horse and reliable as any trooper. It could also be stubborn and hot-tempered, which is why Mullone also nicknamed it *Tintrí:* Fiery-tempered.

'Good boy, *Tintrí.* Good boy.' He patted its neck and ran a hand through its mane. It whickered a contented reply.

There were some livestock being herded across a field and women and children planting seeds and picking early berries.

'They just carry on as if the uprising was somewhere else,' Cahill observed with a disdainful shake of his head. Like the rest of the dragoons, the peak of his helmet cast pools of shadow around his eyes.

'Why shouldn't they?' Mullone answered. 'They still need to eat, to feed their families and cattle, and make money at the markets.'

A tall woman, face partly obscured by a wide slouch hat and the hem of her skirts caked with mud, momentarily glanced up at the horsemen, and Cahill gave an appreciative grunt at her natural beauty.

The sergeant then began to whistle a tuneless rendition of The Rambling Labourer, which Mullone knew was also known as The Girl I left Behind Me. He stopped, face bright with sudden mirth, and then went serious. 'I know someone in New Ross who could be Black, sir. Yes, they could well be the one we're after.'

Mullone tore his gaze from the glorious landscape. 'Oh?' he said, with a raised eyebrow at the sergeant's dubious statement. The horses' hooves thumped dully in the still air.

'Aye, sir, I've been married to her for many years,' Cahill replied with a cackle. He was gap-toothed, small, but stocky and well-muscled and could outride, outshoot and outfight any man that Mullone knew.

'Is that right?' Mullone said with a straight face.

'Aye, sir,' Cahill insisted. 'She's a wee wicked witch, so she is. Mouth like a knife and that woman could talk the teeth out of a saw.'

'Marriage is a sacred virtue, Seán,' Mullone sounded disappointed.

'Aye, and so said the priest that married us,' Cahill replied with another cackle, 'and he was drunk as a lord.'

'You must have loved her once then?' Mullone said drily.

The veteran grinned. 'That's funny, because she says that too.'

'I see that Coveny has the beginnings of a black eye,' Mullone turned to the sergeant. 'Do you know anything about that?'

Cahill shrugged. 'Well, sir, you see that Trooper Coveny has a rare taste for the ladies, and when he's had a few drops of whiskey in him, he becomes very amorous. I was lucky enough to find him in the early hours before he caused any mischief.'

'So how did he get the black eye?'

'He took a tumble on the path back to his quarters, sir,' Cahill said innocently. 'A very nasty path in the dark. Especially treacherous when your mind is swimming with the local moonshine.'

'It was lucky you were there to help him.'

'Aye, sir. A proper blessing, so it was.'

'Coveny needs to be more careful, Seán,' Mullone said.

'Oh, he knows that now, sir. Drink is a curse, I told him. It makes you fight with your good neighbour. It makes you shoot at your landlord and as sure as there is a God, it makes you miss him. I'll tell Coveny that you asked after him, sir.' He gave the major a surreptitious grin at the levity, before hawking and spitting a thick gobbet of green-brown phlegm over the hedgerow.

Mullone knew full well that Cahill had dragged the trooper away before he had made a nuisance of himself in the inn last night that Moore had established for billeting, and for punishment had thumped him. Mullone would let any further recriminations pass, because Cahill was a good sergeant who kept the men in order.

Mullone was the senior officer and the only other subaltern that the regiment now possessed was Lieutenant Michael McBride, who trotted silently behind the two men. Mullone recognised that his young lieutenant had sympathies with the rebel cause, but he was content to leave him alone respecting another man's opinions. Besides, McBride was no threat; he did not openly praise the insurrection, or was swept away with French Revolutionary ideals. He had proved himself an able officer and the men liked him.

'We're just about to come to the town of Naas, sir,' McBride said, crinkled map in hand. 'It's been in all the papers. Utter bloodshed.'

'I heard about it,' Mullone replied to his hollow-cheeked junior officer. A force of rebels, a thousand strong, stormed the town, but were defeated by cannons that blasted grapeshot into their packed ranks. Unable to outflank the soldiers, the insurgents retreated outside and lost a great deal of men to a vengeful troop of sabre-armed cavalry. 'If the Militia hadn't brought up the guns, we'd have lost the town.'

'That's not what I meant, sir,' McBride answered respectfully, but somehow managed to convey that the major's answer was unsatisfactory.

'I know what you implied, Michael,' Mullone said, snapping his head around to address the lieutenant. 'What about Prosperous? The Militia were hacked to death in their beds. One of the officers was younger than your brother Hugh.'

'Repression brings out the worst in people, sir,' McBride muttered, bright sunlight reflected in his spectacles.

Mullone understood that perhaps he had been wrong about him. He would try to talk to him and get the truth out once and for all. If he confessed to being a rebel partisan, then he would be expelled from the regiment in secret in case any rank and file harboured thoughts of mutiny.

'The fields look so charming and green,' Cahill interrupted. 'It is only when you ride through them that you realise they're covered in shit.'

Mullone considered that Cahill understood McBride's feelings too. 'I think you'd better save your breath, Lieutenant. We've still a way to go yet and trouble may interfere with our mission.'

McBride could not meet his gaze, or bring himself to vent his views, and so he stared back at the map.

'What do we do if we come across trouble, sir?' Cahill asked, slapping at a fly. 'As much as I enjoy giving the rebel turds a walloping, it should be down to the Militia to keep the buggers in check.'

'They are doing their job,' Mullone said, glancing at a free-standing Celtic Cross that had once been a prominent feature beside the road, but was now strangled with weeds, besieged with dark moss and deeply pitted with age.

'If you call plundering, fighting and torture work, sir.'

'You don't have much faith in the peace talks then, Seán?'

'No, sir. There's more chance of me taking holy orders and becoming the Pope than there is of peace,' Cahill replied. 'The negotiations that spout from the politicians mouths are nothing but wet farts.'

Mullone chuckled.

'Some men don't want peace,' McBride uttered before he could stop himself.

Mullone scratched at an insect bite on his neck. 'Aye, that's true.'

'People just like Colonel Black, sir,' Cahill muttered. 'He's poked the shit with his sword and raised a stink. So what do we do if there's trouble?'

But then before anyone could answer, a musket shot echoed from the vicinity of Naas and the sergeant grinned like a fed fox.

Mullone closed his eyes. 'Too late.'

*

'Where are the pikes, croppie!' a gravel-voiced sergeant said, as he hauled a man up towards his grizzled face. The man gasped and tried to wrench himself free, but the sergeant was a powerful man, and he could not force himself away.

'There are no weapons here,' he said in desperation, 'not since the fight.'

'You lying croppie bastard!' the sergeant replied and thumped the man with his right fist. 'Do you take me for an idiot? There was a copse here five days ago, and someone has felled the trees to make the pike shafts.'

'No!'

The sergeant was a dark-eyed bullock of a man, and his chin was blue-black with a week's stubble. He took the man over to where the redcoats had boiled up a foul liquid in a squat cauldron above a fire. The town's square was packed with civilians, soldiers and horses. A woman screamed as she was being dragged by her hair away from her house. A dog was barking madly. A musket banged and two mounted officers ordered a platoon of redcoats into the tavern where more men were pushed and hauled out.

A young officer with a cleft chin emerged from the inn with the angry landlord in tow. A young boy, with a running sore on his cheek, darted out of the way. 'This fellow claims that none of the ringleaders have come back since the fight, sir,' he said to an observing grey-haired officer mounted on a well-groomed chestnut horse.

The single gold epaulette on his right shoulder indicated the older officer was a captain, and he urged his mount forwards with a touch of his steel spurs at its flanks.

'Where's the priest?' he bawled, through a bushy gun metal-grey moustache.

The innkeeper, who had thick side-whiskers and receding hair, shrugged.

'We are after a priest who calls himself Father Keay,' the captain revealed. 'Red hair, beard to match and he carries a sword. I know he was one of the ringleaders who led the attack on our outposts here, and I know he was seen at Ballitore two days ago and here again yesterday. Now where is he?'

'I don't know of that priest,' the innkeeper replied. 'I see lots of new folk on the roads. Some stable their horses and leave the next day, but I don't know of that man, sir. I've not seen him here.'

The captain stared into the man's fearful eyes and he knew he was telling the truth. But someone here had seen the priest, or knew of him, and this man would serve as an example to the onlookers.

'Sergeant Nolan.'

'Sir?' the dark-eyed soldier answered.

'Bind this man and take him to the cauldron. Let's see if the hot tar loosens some tongues around here.'

Nolan grinned wickedly. 'My pleasure, sir.'

The wretched man was dragged away and taken to where the black liquid bubbled and spat. The landlord, a rope-maker and a wheelwright had their hands bound behind their backs and positioned on their knees by a Militia private each. Nolan then began the terrible torture known as 'pitch-capping'. He ladled hot pitch into three waxed paper caps and, as the men tried to resist their captors, Nolan forced a cap onto each of their heads. They screamed; heads twisted in agony, tears rolled down their cheeks. Nolan stood grinning as the sticky liquid simmered and cooled upon their crowns.

A woman, possibly one of the victim's wives, screeched for clemency, but she was ignored and fell weeping to the ground. An old man, white-bearded and skeletal, tried to push past the redcoats to help the three kneeling victims, but was knocked down and kicked into unconsciousness.

A moment later, amidst the tormented shrieking, Nolan stooped over the wriggling men and ripped off the caps; tearing away hair and skin in the process. Their crowns were blistered and raw and would leave them disfigured like victims of scalping.

'Now bring me the shears,' Nolan said in a harsh, throaty voice. A grinning private brought him a pair of crude scissors. 'This is what happens to lying croppie bastards,' he said using the moniker that had been first given to Irish rebels who had cropped their hair in the French Revolutionary style in protest at the aristocratic long hair and wigs. Now it was now applied to all suspects of the rebellion. The scissors made short work of the remaining stubs of hair. Nolan drew blood as he sheared the heads, clipping the top of the wheelwright's ear, and raking the sore skin without deliberation.

'Bring the innkeeper's daughter forward,' the captain demanded, 'and we'll see if that will loosen some tongues.' The officer behind him, a lieutenant with brown crooked teeth and warts on his chin, grinned.

'What's going on here?' a voice bellowed with such irrefutable authority that the lieutenant twisted in his saddle, saluted immediately.

The moustached captain looked across the road, scowling at the interruption. 'Who the devil are you?' he asked with much intended impudence. He saw a blond-haired officer with a red sweat-stained face and perhaps forty dragoons. They wore Tarleton crested helmets with a turban in the same grass green as their facings. The men looked like a Yeomanry unit, who, in the captain's mind, were not proper soldiers. However, the horsemen were hard-faced, grim and looked as though they had honed their skills in battle.

'Major Lorn Mullone of Lord Lovell's Dragoons,' replied the officer who trotted towards him. His plume bobbled in motion to the horse's stride. 'Who are you, sir?' he asked coldly.

'Captain Torrington.'

Mullone stared at the pale yellow facings on the men's coats. 'Ennis Torrington of the North Wicklow County Militia?'

Torrington seemed to brighten up as his reputation was evident. 'Yes,' he offered a slight bow in the saddle.

'Lieutenant James Foote, sir,' said the brown-toothed officer.

'Be quiet and leave us,' Mullone snapped and the lieutenant's gaze swivelled to his captain as though seeking approval. Mullone leaned in closer. 'Are your ears full of straw, boy? I ordered you to leave.'

Torrington twitched as the lieutenant made a feeble departure.

Mullone looked past him and shook his head at the mayhem beyond. He could see the fear in the people's eyes.

'What's that ungodly smell, sir?' asked Cahill, sniffing like a hog.

'Pitch-capping, Seán.'

'Sweet Jesus,' the sergeant crossed himself at the stench of burnt flesh.

'I've seen far worse than this,' Mullone said. 'I've seen them sprinkle gunpowder, or soak the pitch in turpentine first, and then set the caps alight.'

'It's certainly an effective method,' Torrington replied with apparent satisfaction. 'I also use the travelling gallows when I can,' he pointed at a horrid contraption next to two wagons. It had two solid wheels and two frames that resembled a simple farm cart but up-ended. A thick strip of rope was nailed between the frames so that a noosed prisoner could be lynched on the spot. Two redcoats would steady the frames and up to four privates would pull on the rope, thus pulling the bound man up over the nailed rope to slowly choke until he confessed. 'A throttling sets a good example, but it's the hot tar that everyone fears. It's the tried and tested method to get results.'

Mullone said nothing. Instead, he seemed preoccupied with the hanging device, for his eyes glassed over, staring at it in deep thought. 'It's utterly barbaric.'

Torrington sniffed derisively as though he found the major weak. 'I know that trees were cut down to make pike shafts and the pike heads will be buried under the gardens, or in false graves and walls, or tucked up in whores' filthy skirts.' He gave Mullone a foul grin to make him uncomfortable. 'I'll dig up the gardens, I'll pull down walls, and I'll force the whores' legs wider apart to inspect their notches. I will find the weapons. I can assure you of that.'

'What about simply talking to the people?'

Torrington scoffed. 'What use is that? Might as well converse with animals, or the moon. You can accomplish more with a stout shillelagh than you can with words.'

'"*For all they that take the sword, shall perish with the sword*",' Mullone recited the parable causing the captain to scowl at him.

'Torrington, just because there are one or two bad apples in the crop, it doesn't mean the whole orchard is rotten.'

Torrington gave a guttural grunt of amusement. 'You men from the Castle are as soft as fresh butter.'

'We're certainly more compassionate.'

The captain wrinkled his face, pulled out a canteen of brandy and guzzled it back without offering any to Mullone. 'Life does not exist without authority,' he said, wiping the spirit from the ends of his drooping moustache. 'Out here it is men like me that give the government its power. I keep the peace and punish the guilty. The government in return pays me. I am rather shocked at your naivety on the matter.'

'The word, Torrington, when you address me,' Mullone said menacingly, 'is "sir".'

Anger sparked in the captain's eyes, but he bit his lip at whatever he was about to quickly retort. 'Sir,' he said with displeasure.

Mullone smiled at him triumphantly.

Cahill watched Nolan pull an attractive woman from the crowd towards the bubbling cauldron. Her hands were tied. He clicked his horse forward.

'Now, my pretty one, hold still while I put this nice cap on you,' Nolan said, as the woman screamed and begged him to stop.

'Da! Help me!'

Nolan chortled. 'Your da's not in a position to help you.'

A private handed Nolan the cap, but suddenly a horse knocked him flat over and the sergeant craned his neck up to look into a weather-hewn face that marked the cavalryman as a seasoned campaigner. 'Who the hell are you?'

'A man who's about to beat the seven casks of shit out of you,' replied Cahill. 'Let the pretty lady go,' he said, dismounting.

The prone redcoat tried to get to his feet, but Cahill kicked him in the face. Nolan pushed the woman to the ground and reached for the sword hanging at his left hip.

'If you draw that, you bastard,' Cahill warned him, 'I'll kill you before you can scratch your shrivelled prick with it.'

Nolan brayed as the blade rasped free. 'I'll use your stinking corpse for shooting practice after I spill your rotten guts.'

'Are you going to permit this, Major?' Torrington reeled. 'I won't have my men made fools of.'

Mullone patted *Tintreach's* sweat-lathered neck, his eyes jumping up to Cahill. 'My sergeant is only defending himself, Torrington,' he said icily, 'or do you have no stomach to watch when fighting someone who is not helpless and unarmed?'

Torrington's shoulders went taut. 'Damn you,' he murmured.

'I will not be a party to torture,' Mullone said. 'There is rarely any reason to torture women.'

'They can tell me something that may help with my enquiries.'

Mullone shot Torrington a look of disdain. 'Do you care about nothing?'

'I care about apprehending rebels.'

Nolan lunged and whipped the dull iron sword up towards his foe's face, but Cahill dodged the attack with fluid ease and let out a laugh. He had not drawn his own blade yet.

'Christ on His bloody cross, no wonder the croppies have got you running around in circles.'

'A friend to them, are you?' Nolan sneered, slashing again.

'Better them than you,' Cahill retorted.

'I've killed enough of 'em,' Nolan boasted to which Cahill scoffed at the man's hyperbole. Nolan growled. 'So what's one that wears a redcoat worth? I wouldn't wipe my arse on your stinking rags!'

The crowd, swollen by people who had come from their houses, cheered Cahill, and he returned their appreciative shouts with a wave.

'Always the entertainer,' Mullone muttered.

Nolan grunted as he feinted left, cut right and was pleasantly surprised to slice open Cahill's left forearm. He laughed at Cahill's look of indignation and surprise.

Cahill staggered backwards as though he had resigned himself to early defeat and Nolan roared as he sprang forward. But it was all a feint and Cahill kicked him hard between the legs. Nolan collapsed. Cahill punched him in the throat and slapped the sword out of his hands. Then he grabbed Nolan by his powdered hair and ran him over to the simmering cauldron.

'No!' Nolan gasped and although he was taller and bulkier than Cahill, he did not possess his strength. Cahill tipped him over the cauldron's rim pushing his face closer to the steaming liquid. Nolan gripped the rim with his bare hands and screamed as his fingers and palms were seared.

'Stop this at once!' Torrington ordered Cahill, ignoring Mullone.

Cahill expected to be dragged off by now, but no one came to Nolan's aid, which proved that he was not liked by his own men. A man from the crowd swore at the Militia. Their faces stirred with nervousness and remained inactive even when one member of the crowd threw stones at them.

Nolan attempted one final push to break free, but Cahill punched him in the kidneys and banged his head hard against the cauldron's thick rim, which rang like a bell. His screams were cut off as his face plunged into the scolding liquid. Cahill held him there with his iron-muscled arms until Mullone ordered him to let him go.

'That's enough, Seán.'

'Aye, sir,' Cahill obeyed and Nolan dropped to the ground like a heavy stone tumbled into a well, writhing in agony, with smoke coming from the pits of his boiled eyes and shrivelled nose. Cahill blew the horrid stench away from his face. He cut the woman's bonds with a knife, mounted his horse and waved to the woman, who in turn blew him a kiss.

'Are you all right?' Mullone asked his friend as he trotted back.

'Aye, sir. Blade just cut the sleeve.'

'I'll have you cashiered for this!' Torrington said furiously.

Mullone said nothing for a moment, but then seemed unable to control the anger, his blood up. 'You'll do not such thing, sir! I know who you are! You should be patrolling Wicklow, not Kildare. What are you doing this far north?'

'I was ordered here, Major,' Torrington replied as though he found the questions insulting.

'By whose authority?'

'I have written papers.'

'From who, damn you?'

'General Sir Ralph Dundas.' The Militia captain pulled out the said papers from inside his jacket. 'He has exercised caution and consolidated my men with Militia from Kildare and Queens County in rounding up a known ringleader called Father Keay. A villainous priest who preaches seditious sermons. He was seen here yesterday.' He handed the orders to Mullone who read them eagerly.

Sir Ralph, the district commander, had signed the papers and there was nothing Mullone could do to stop Torrington's movements. But there were questions that he could certainly answer.

'You were recently acquainted with a certain person in Wicklow. Is that correct?'

Torrington snorted. 'Colonel Black?'

'Aye.'

'Has the army gone soft and sent you to round him up?'

Mullone's face was taut. 'I asked you a question.'

'And I asked you one,' Torrington said obstinately. 'Don't try to play games with me, Major. I was killing the king's enemies when you were still sucking your mother's teats. When I wasn't employed by His Majesty, I was killing enemies in the name of William, Prince of Orange. Now, are you after Black?'

Mullone bit his lower lip, sighed and went against his better judgement. 'That is my assignment,' he replied levelly, thrusting the papers back.

Torrington ordered his company to form up. 'I met the man south of a village called Shillelagh when we caught cattle-boats loaded with arms as they made their way north to Hacketstown,' he revealed. The hanging contraption was noisily loaded onto one of the carts with the seriously injured Nolan. 'I know nothing else about Black.'

'Could you describe him?'

Torrington played with the ends of his moustache. 'Black hair, blue eyes, and not loquacious, but when he did, he was well-spoken like a true gentleman.'

The one thing Mullone had learned from his years of campaigning was that there was nothing gentlemanly about war. Nothing whatsoever.

'How many men did he have with him?'

'Fifty,' Torrington hazarded a guess.

'Dragoons?'

'Aye.'

'Anything else you can tell me about him?'

'I never caught his first name if that's what you're asking for,' Torrington mocked. 'As I said, he wasn't very talkative. He asked me to assist him in dealing with some of the rebel scum.'

'Did he say what he was doing?'

Torrington studied Mullone for a moment. 'No, he did not. But…'

'But what?'

'I overhead him talking to his captain about losing two of his men in the mountains near Oldbridge.' Torrington took off his bicorn hat, which had left a greasy rim-mark in his hair, and scratched. 'Something about pursuing a blacksmith who had some dealings with Father Keay, the priest I'm after. Maybe the smith had something to do with the deaths of Black's men?' He shrugged and rammed the hat back on. 'I don't know.'

'Is that all?'

'Aye.'

'A cavalry troop been spotted near New Ross,' Mullone said. 'I think it's Black. Do you know why he would travel all that way there?'

'To find the blacksmith?' Torrington sounded exasperated. 'Or the priest?' He pinched the bridge of his nose as though the conversation was testing his patience. 'Whatever Black is doing, Major,' he said with a crooked smile, 'it's for the better of Ireland.'

'What?' Mullone said incredulously.

'Death to all traitors of the king. Is that not what Pitt wants? I wouldn't hand him over for a thousand guineas.'

Mullone gave that comment the look it deserved before leaving.

'Jesus and all the saints,' Cahill remarked, as he reined in on the grassy crest of Corbet Hill, overlooking the towering walls of New Ross.

The town was pretty; set in a picturesque location on the banks of the River Barrow that was bursting with plump cargo boats, gun boats and skiffs. Mullone could see the quay where a long wooden bridge spanned over the glassy, smoke-coloured river to the neighbouring port-town of Rosbercon. New Ross was protected by an imposing semi-circular wall that included five great gates and nine flanking towers. If there ever was a siege; it appeared to be hard-pressed to break down those unsullied defences.

Cahill whistled. 'That'd be a tough bastard to storm.'

'Thankfully, we won't have to,' Mullone replied.

But as Mullone followed the winding grassy track down the precipitous hill, he noticed that the mossy walls and turrets were crumbling, and the gates were defenceless. He also realised Corbet's Hill dominated the entire area, so that any enemies could see where the defenders were placed in any part of the town; almost a bird's-eye view. There was nowhere to conceal the troops unless kept hidden in the small houses. He wondered why no redcoats garrisoned the hill and no artillery batteries were emplaced to guard the roads. Surely that was key in the defence of the town?

About a hundred labourers, supervised by an officer, were digging trenches outside the most easterly gate. Mullone saw that his scarlet coat had two gold epaulettes revealing his rank was either a major, a lieutenant-colonel, or a colonel. He looked up, hearing the hoof beats and watched their arrival with suspicion.

'Major Mullone, sir,' he said, saluting, having an inkling that he was the officer, Moore had asked him to report to. 'Lord Lovell's Dragoons.'

The officer replied the salute almost guardedly. He was a small man with a thin face, in his mid-thirties and the sight of the horseman seemed to bother him, for he was silent for a moment as he studied faces, equipment and horse furniture.

'Where are you from?' he asked, sizing Mullone up with a look of irritation laced with bewilderment. His accent betrayed that he was Scottish.

'Colonel Moore sent me from Dublin, sir,' Mullone replied. 'Would you be Colonel Craufurd?'

'I am,' he said, scowling. 'Moore wrote to me to say he was sending a government man. He also said you'd arrive two days ago. I assumed you were dead. What the devil kept you, Major? Got lost?'

'Apologies, sir. Business in Ulster,' Mullone said as carefully as he dared.

Craufurd gave an imperceptible nod at the uninformative reply. 'There's always business in Ulster,' he snapped. 'You can stable your horses at the old blacksmith's on Neville Street.' He pointed down the cramped road that was packed with a Militia regiment marching north towards where the spire of an abbey loomed above thatched roofs. 'Take the first left. You'll find the smithy near the barracks on Michaels Lane. Major-General Johnson commands this city. I will inform him of your arrival. He'll want to know why. Not sure why Moore would send us more cavalry,' he said ungratefully. 'No bloody good against pikes. What we need is infantry and guns. Do your men know how to fight?'

'Yes, sir.'

'Good. Dinner at eight at the Quayhouse Inn.' He said the last sentence as a command rather than an invitation.

'Thank you, sir.'

'Ignore the band of fools with the firearms inside the gate; the eldest sons of prominent land owners. Keen, but no common sense of their generation. Don't let me keep you,' Craufurd dismissed him to supervise the placements of two six-pounders near the entryway, which Mullone heard him call Three Bullet Gate. It had been widened with pickaxes and chisels to allow two lanes of wagons and carts to pass through it.

A hail of pistol and carbine fire shredded the air as young men on horseback discharged their weapons skyward. They whooped and laughed. They were watched by a unit of blue-coated horsemen with very grave expressions. Mullone shot the commander a look of pity.

'Idiots,' Lieutenant McBride muttered at the youths in their wealthy clothes.

'They just need a good thrashing with a strip of birch,' Cahill replied. 'I'd do it for nothing.'

Mullone led his men on; the horses' hooves were loud on the cobbled street that was stained with horse urine and dung. A lieutenant marching a platoon of men towards the gate saluted Mullone. A woman looked down on them through a window as they trotted past. Cahill looked up, saw her and waved. She shot him a withering look, made the sign of the cross, and went back inside.

'You've got that effect on most people, Sergeant,' Mullone said.

'That's the wife, sir,' Cahill said and cackled. He took a lungful of dung-filled air. 'Home sweet home.'

'She reminds me of my girl,' said Corporal Brennan, a long clay pipe clamped between his teeth.

'Jesus. How so?' Cahill raised an eyebrow.

'Feisty-looking, Sergeant,' Brennan said with a wink. He was nicknamed Black-Eyed Brennan, for his eyes were like polished orbs of jet. He blew a large pall of pungent smoke into the air above him. 'My Nora took care of herself when the croppies tried to take Clondalkin. One tried to have his wicked way with her, but he never saw the knife she used to geld him with.' The dark-eyed corporal laughed. 'Gelded him like a pig. Aye, a pig! She's a lovely wee thing.'

'And maybe one day she'll cut out your tongue and do us all a goddamn favour,' Cahill replied dryly.

Brennan looked wounded. 'Now where would you be without my heart-warming stories, Sergeant?'

'Happy,' Cahill remarked with gap-toothed grin. A woman was walking up the road carrying a basket of bread and the sergeant whistled. 'Now that's a fine form!'

'She can shine my privy member anytime,' Coveny sniggered and the woman blushed.

'Quiet back there,' Mullone's voice shattered the gales of laughter.

'Some fine ale and a soft bed will do me tonight,' a pox-scarred trooper named O'Shea said, rubbing his sore behind.

'Never mind that,' Cahill grumbled. 'I want some decent hot food for a change. No more salt beef and hard bread.'

A boy and two girls played in the street ahead of the dragoons and their mother dashed out of her thatched home, clutching all three in her arms, before taking them inside. The boy broke free and gave Mullone a salute. The major smiled, and happily returned the greeting.

'They say the people of New Ross are very loyal to the king,' McBride said, as they passed a row of simple wooden houses where a Union Flag had been crudely etched into one of the beams.

'More loyal than you Dubliners, sir,' Cahill replied proudly.

Mullone said nothing, because as they rounded the street, something caught his eye. A corpse was hanging from one of the street lamps opposite the barracks. He was long dead, and as they trotted closer, Mullone could see a strip of parchment was tied around his neck. Remnants of clothes hung ragged from the yellowed bones.

Cahill leaned in. '"A just end to a traitor",' he read out aloud. He stared at the cadaver and grunted in disgust. 'Got what he deserved. Bugger was a turncoat,' he pointed a dirty finger at the tattered coat that was turned inside to show the mark of dishonour.

Traitor.

Mullone knuckled his forehead. The image of the young man swinging from a gallows pierced his vision again. It was too much for him. He turned away, a sourness showing on his usually affable face.

'Move on,' he barked, tugging savagely on *Tintreach's* reins.

It was beginning to have an effect. The past was plaguing him. Mullone had to tell someone soon. Cahill would be the first to know.

But for now his mission was his only purpose. He was also painfully aware that the horses needed a proper rest; he was tired and saddle-sore, and would need to freshen up for tonight to dine in unfamiliar company. He groaned, thinking of the small talk and, if Craufurd was the martinet he was renowned for being, tonight could be even more draining than the long journey from Ulster.

In the morning he would ride out to find Black and complete his mission.

For Moore had sent a killer to catch a killer.

In the early hours of the morning, Mullone returned to his billet which was a spacious airy room in the Customs House overlooking the quay. His head was swimming with claret and his belly aching from rich sumptuous food that was served on best china. He had eaten a delicious stew, a breast of mutton and wolfed down delicious sugared cakes for afters. The officers had then smoked cigars, drank brandy, talked about the rebellion and shared news from all corners of the country.

Cahill and the other men had been content to drink ale, eat oysters, salt-beef and oatcakes. They were not permitted to leave the smithy. Mullone did not want any of them to get drunk and aggravate the townsfolk. Craufurd would be on him like a terrier on a rat.

General Henry Johnson turned out to be an energetic, pleasant man of fifty with a fleshy face and generous mouth. He had fought with Cornwallis against the Americans and was pleased to find that Mullone had also fought there and wanted to know more of his military background, much to Mullone's chagrin for he disliked talking about that particular conflict. Craufurd was present, as well as a host of Militia officers from Kildare, Donegal and Lord Mountjoy. Luke Gardiner, Viscount Mountjoy was a colonel of a Dublin Militia regiment, and had entered the town ahead of his marching column, two artillery pieces and a Scottish mounted Fencible regiment, to the excited cheers, waves and whistles of the townsfolk.

Morale, Johnson pompously exclaimed, was extremely high and Lord Mountjoy said he was honoured to be present.

'God, will let us prevail,' he said piously.

'I hope He will, sir,' Mullone said.

Lord Mountjoy thought he was being mocked. His head spun to fix a drilling stare at the major. 'Do you believe in God, sir?'

Mullone paused before speaking. 'There are times when I believe in nothing more than a loaded carbine and a newly-honed blade, sir. But to answer your question, yes, I do.'

Mountjoy pursed his lips. 'Good,' he said curtly and decided not to press Mullone any further. He turned to Johnson. 'The good Lord will protect us behind these stout walls. God is our refuge and our strength from any attack.'

'An imminent attack,' Johnson commented to the dozen or more men.

A Militia captain, brandy in hand, seemed to stagger with the threat. 'I thought we had a week at least, sir?'

Johnson shook his head vehemently. 'I wish that were so. Thousands of insurgents have reached Carrickbyrne Hill.' Carrickbyrne was ten miles to the west, a day's march away. 'They've had the audacity to request that I surrender the town.'

The Militia captain's neck convulsed as he swallowed quickly. 'God preserve us!'

'Be quiet,' Craufurd admonished him.

'They say that only by surrendering will it save the town from rapine and plunder to the ruin of the innocent,' Johnson continued, and gave a small ironic laugh. 'They came under a flag of truce. So I allowed the messenger to leave with a firm and unequivocal 'no'.

'And damn their nerve, sir,' Craufurd rose a glass to him.

Johnson paused and looked serious. 'In truth, I've lost all communication with Captain Tait and his men at Scullabogue. Alas, I do not have accurate numbers. A thousand have been spotted north crossing the River Nore, so I have placed gunboats to watch the estuary for movement and as many men as I can spare to watch the roads, hills and outer villages.'

'How many rebels were counted at Carrickbyrne, sir?' Mullone enquired.

Johnson cleared his throat and sipped rich claret before answering. 'Between fifteen and twenty thousand.'

The room went deathly silent. One of the long candles popped and uniform wearing servants returned with more port and claret.

Mullone imagined the hordes of pikemen storming through the gates, the lightly-numbered red-coated lines firing into them, volley after volley. It would take nerves of steel to stand firm against such a horde.

'Confirmed, sir?' Mullone asked.

Johnson chewed the inside of a cheek. 'Fairly mixed reports, but there you have it.'

It was dispiriting to know the enemy possibly numbered ten times their own number, but Craufurd looked calm and a couple of the officers were staring at him for inspiration.

'Our men will beat them,' the small colonel said with easy confidence. 'I have no other convictions on the matter. Disciplined troops will always beat an untrained mob. No matter how many of them there are.'

'Agreed!' replied a captain of a blue-coated Yeomanry attachment. He was ruddy-faced with raised veins on his cheeks and nose. 'They won't stand.'

'There will be women and children in the rabble,' said another, a young man, barely into his twenties, but swayed with an air of confidence that Mullone knew immediately was born of wealth and privilege. 'You can't include them in that number who can fight.'

'Agreed,' Craufurd said, his mouth pressed into a hard line.

The officer turned to the Scotsmen. 'What you need is to funnel the rest into the streets where there will be no hope of getting out alive. Only that way will we win.'

'Don't begin to tell me what to do,' Craufurd growled. 'Leave the strategies to those with merit, and not their parents' money.'

The young officer, seemingly unconcerned by the retort, turned to his companions with a smile and a shrug.

Johnson turned to Mullone. 'I am aware of your duties, but will you stay and fight with us, Major?' he asked, and the rest of the officers waited eagerly for Mullone's answer. 'You command a troop, I know, but we could use the help of your rogues. What do you say?'

Mullone sipped claret. Truthfully, he did not want to stay and help defend the town. He had a mission to complete, an order from the Viceroy himself. However, he was a soldier at heart, and had fought for king and country for over thirty years.

'Of course, sir,' he said.

Johnson slapped his shoulder in joy. 'Capital, my dear friend, capital!'

'Concentrated volley fire and artillery support will see the insurgents off,' Craufurd commented further, and Mullone had felt he had said it to counter any negative thoughts in the room – particularly to a handful of Militia officers who seemed to still be cowering from the reports. 'We'll teach them that insurrection buys the price of a grave. The others will melt away like snow fall on a hot spring day.'

Returning to his billet, Mullone had not felt Craufurd's confidence and now as he tugged off his boots, stripped naked and climbed wearily into his bed, he felt anxious and wanted nothing more to ride out with his men to hunt down Black.

It was stiflingly hot, even with the windows open, but Mullone still shivered. He pulled the covers closer and tried to sleep.

The next morning he was roused by a cheerful Sergeant Cahill who brought him breakfast of cooked eggs, bread and a pot of coffee. He dressed before venturing outside on the wooden balcony, taking in the crisp sweet air.

'Morning, sir,' Cahill said. 'A grand day, so it is.'

Mullone rubbed his eyes and groaned. 'It is?' An oxbow moon was visible above the tiled roof and the sunlight glimmered on the river's surface like a mirror.

'Yes, sir.'

Mullone had not slept well. He had dreamt of the town burning. Of his men cut down, of Black laughing and of the hanging man again.

'I have brought you some papers, sir,' Cahill said, wafting the creased papers under Mullone's nose. 'They're both three days old, but I know how you like to read them with your breakfast. There are some terrible stories that Black has struck again. A family including their three children nailed to a barn door whilst they were still alive. Not far from here too.'

Mullone fixed him a shocked look. 'Dear God!' He fought against a yawn and lost. 'I'll read them in a minute, Seán.'

'Late night, sir,' Cahill said with mock sympathy.

'Something like that,' Mullone shared a smile and watched the fishermen out on the water. He couldn't see the gunboats and reckoned they had left for the north in the night as Johnson had advised.

'You weren't still thinking about that deserter, were you?' Cahill asked.

Mullone rubbed his cheeks, and glanced awkwardly at him. 'What do you mean?'

Cahill shrugged. 'It's just that it's not the first time I've seen you bothered by a hanging corpse.' The sergeant leaned closer and Mullone smelt ale on his breath and stale pipe tobacco on his uniform. 'I never mentioned it before, but I've heard you mention the name Solomon under your breath a few times. Who is he, if you don't mind me asking, sir?'

Mullone drank some coffee and said nothing for a moment, as though the very thought of answering choked the breath from him.

'Solomon was my brother,' he said eventually. 'He was my twin and he died.'

'I'm sorry, sir,' Cahill suddenly regretted his enquiry.

Mullone sipped the coffee. 'We had enlisted together. When we were fighting the Americans he fell in love with a girl and deserted to the rebels to start a new life.'

'Oh,' the sergeant pursed his lips and blew a lungful of breath. 'Turned his coat for love, sir?'

'Yes.'

'And they killed him?'

'No,' Mullone said recalling the events. 'Solomon had run away to be with her and I had gone as far as I could with them before saying goodbye. I was angry and upset, because I couldn't change his mind. But he was happy and that's what all that mattered.' Mullone took a breath to cover the sadness. It had been sad to see Solomon leave, because they were very close. They had both been sent to Seville to study for priesthood, but had gone against their parent's wishes and decided to join the army for adventure. 'We were fighting Washington's army in Philadelphia when Solomon was caught trying to escape across the lines. He was hung as a traitor.'

Cahill softened his tone. 'Jesus, I'm sorry, sir.'

'It was twenty years ago,' Mullone said, 'but I can't stop thinking about him of late. I should have stopped him. People said he was weak, but do you know that he was actually the strong one? He left everything behind for love. I couldn't have done that. He knew what he wanted in life. I regret letting him go, in my dreams I cling onto him, but when I wake up, the truth hits me. It's as though I sent him to his doom.'

'It wasn't your fault, sir,' Cahill said loyally. 'Your brother knew what he was doing, he knew the risks. And ever since you've been beating yourself up over that?'

Mullone's eyes were riveted to the ripples in the swirling water below. 'Yes.'

'I think you need to let him go, sir. It's unhealthy to keep blaming yourself for something beyond your control.'

'I should have stopped him, Seán,' Mullone said, voice loud enough to startle two coots and moorhens that splashed away in alarm.

Cahill scratched the bristles on his chin. 'You weren't to know what would happen to him. We can't change the past, sir. No matter how wonderful it would be to do so.'

'I see him a lot now and I think he's trying to tell me something.'

Cahill's expression was as wrinkled as an old apple. 'Sir?'

'This,' Mullone said, holding out a hand. There was a small silver cross on a chain. He couldn't explain it, but it had something to do with it. After his brother's death, he had questioned his faith and walked a very rocky path for many years. At the beginning of the war against France, he started to look for salvation and now he reckoned that Solomon was telling him not to give up, to hold onto his faith. It would take some time, but he was healing slowly.

'Sir,' Cahill struggled to find the words. 'I…'

'It doesn't matter.' Mullone drank some coffee, feeling its richness stir life into his limbs. He noticed that the sergeant's left sleeve was crudely stitched up from the scuffle with Nolan. 'Our objective is to find Colonel Black.'

'The man's gotten under my skin like a burrowing tick,' Cahill said.

'I can understand that feeling, but we have to help defend the town. The general reckons that the rebels will be here soon. We can't abandon the women and children, so we stay and fight for them. Then, we'll get Black. Tell the men to get themselves ready.'

'Oh, I will, sir,' Cahill said. 'The lads will be looking forward to a wee scrap. Sir?'

'Yes?'

'Let's hope we break some skulls.'

*

It was late in the afternoon when the first rebels were spotted on Corbet Hill. Their arrival had been pre-empted by a huge dust cloud that whitened the sky. The picquets had returned back to the town before noon to say that the entire horizon, mile after mile, was darkening. The rebels were moving inexorably towards New Ross like the slow-flow of lava.

In truth, the rebel force was swollen with local villagers caught up in the fervour of the march. Thousands of women and children; the camp followers brought up the rear with carts full of oats, mutton, bedding, cooking pots, whiskey and beer. There were scores of home-stitched flags held aloft in proud hands. Drummers, flutists and pipers played their instruments. A few priests marched with their extended congregations, some armed with a myriad of hand weapons, others with simple crosses. The army pressed on towards New Ross like a terrifying pilgrimage, armed with musket and pike, and breathing nothing but vengeance and hatred.

That night Johnson convened a council of war in the Court House, knowing that his rebel counterpart, a man called John Fitzstephen, would be doing the same on the hilltop. He was a descendant of Norman nobility that had arrived in Ireland in the twelfth century. He was passionate, resourceful, beloved, and one of the United Irishman's most charismatic leaders.

Johnson's force of two thousand was mostly Militia with a few hundred regulars, Yeomanry and some cavalry. The horsemen would guard the bridge to Rosbercon, and some would act as aides. He was generally sure of success, but worried about defeat and the safety of his people. His main concern was that enthusiastic men would rush into battle without the true knowledge of its realities. Most recently a force of the North Cork Militia had been wiped out at a place called Oulart Hill, because the men had been eager to engage the enemy, and then were overwhelmed and ripped apart by pikes. Johnson could not afford any losses from over-zealous men.

'Any news, sir?' Mullone enquired. The assembled officers, some thirty or more men, seemed only interested in drinking the fine claret and smoking cigars. Craufurd would join the council later, having spent another day inspecting the defences.

'The latest reports say that the rebels haven't advanced anywhere else,' Johnson replied, as he sifted through the messages sent by commanders and loyal people outside of the town. 'The west is quiet too.'

'No news is good news,' chirped a captain of blue-coated dragoons.

Johnson winced.

'So they're all up there,' breathed the Militia captain that Craufurd had hitherto chided.

'They won't come,' said another officer, voice distorted and face swollen because of an infected tooth. He sipped whiskey in the vain hope of dulling the pain. 'They won't break our walls.'

'They have no firepower,' an artillery officer stroked the ends of his moustache. 'They can't breach the walls.'

But, in their thousands, they could easily swarm the gates, Mullone thought.

He stared down at the crude map of the city that the general had brought with him. It was difficult to make out the town in the spidery ink-drawn lines.

Johnson tapped New Ross with a finger. 'I suspect, along with Colonel Craufurd, that Fitzstephen will launch the first assault against the eastern defences,' he said, jabbing a digit at the Three Bullet Gate. 'I wonder if that priest is up there with him now.'

'Priest, sir?' Mullone asked.

'A clergyman called Keay,' Johnson scoffed.

Mullone's eyes narrowed, recalling the use of the name from Captain Torrington. 'Keay?' he repeated.

'Aye.'

'Do you know much about him, sir? In my lines of enquiry from the Castle, this priest has been mentioned before.'

Irritation flashed on the general's face for an instant, as though he didn't want to be interrupted with unimportant matters. He had a town to save. He rubbed his temples. There were bags of exhaustion under his eyes. 'He's believed to be leading the rebels in this area, and now jointly leads the mob. I don't know much else about him other than he's French, he's a damned upstart and that he is certainly no priest.'

Mullone knew instantly who this was.

De Marin.

Mullone brushed a hand through his hair, convinced even more that he was supposed to be here. De Marin was the French spy that he had tracked to Ulster, but he was more slippery than a wet rat in a gutter, and had somehow evaded capture. He had known of the Frenchman for a number of years and he was a true enemy. The last time he had seen him was at Fishguard and he had escaped before Mullone could apprehend him. And now he was here in Wexford, stirring discontent, and adding fuel to the fire. Mullone would do everything in his power to stop him.

'Sounds like De Marin, sir?' McBride whispered and Mullone gave a determined nod.

Johnson traced a finger down the town's wall, past Mary's Tower to the Priory Gate. He was sure that no rebels would be able to reach that part of the defences, or bother with it, so he would leave it virtually undefended. He positioned the main bulk of the troops and guns at various strong points; the Three Bullet Gate, the barracks, the marketplace, the street known as Main Guard which housed the gaol and the Court House, and finally, the oak bridge which provided a safe retreat out of the town. He would also leave a contingent of reserve troops at the North Gate where they could be brought forward to enforce any weak points or to defend any retreat.

Colonel Craufurd entered the room, calm and quiet, and Mullone studied his eyes that twinkled with intelligence and understanding. He poured himself a drink and edged over to the map whereby Johnson gave him a curt nod.

'The cavalry stays at the quay,' Johnson enforced his previous order to the assembled commanders. 'I don't want the horses clogging up the streets. They won't be able to charge the rebel pikes. Swords have proven useless. They'll be slaughtered, so they're to stay and guard the bridge.'

'Once you get past the point, won't it be easy?' Lord Mountjoy asked and a Militia officer grunted with agreement.

Craufurd, eyes bright in the light, smiled wolfishly. 'But getting past the point is the difficult bit.'

Lord Mountjoy gave a small laugh.

'Unless advised otherwise, the cavalry is to remain at the quay,' Johnson reinforced his order by thumping the table with his fists. 'No cavalry and no goddamn heroics.'

'My men can fight on foot, sir,' Mullone said without boasting and two officers at the back sneered at the remark. Craufurd scowled at them into silence. 'They're dragoons and they can fight as infantrymen.'

Johnson smiled crookedly. 'We'll make use of your carbines, Mullone.'

'Some of the townsfolk have requested to leave their homes, sir,' Craufurd said.

Johnson put up his hands in a sign of peace. 'Let them go, if they so wish.'

Craufurd scratched the blue-black stubble on his chin. 'I've removed the two-dozen 'glory-men', sir.' They were loyal volunteers who were just too hot-headed to have around, so they had been disarmed and confined to their homes for everyone's safety.

'Excellent. I'll not have anyone killed for misplaced bravery.'

'I've also enforced the probation of selling strong drink after nine in the evening on account of the pugilists. Two men have already been arrested for brawling.'

Johnson grunted in abhorrence. 'I may decide to close the liquor shops down until the threats have passed.'

Someone clapped his hands at the order, while another groaned.

'Very good, sir,' Craufurd rejoined, face expressionless. 'What do you want to do with the prisoners in the event of an assault?'

Johnson bit his lip. 'How many does the gaol hold at present?'

'Thirteen, sir,' replied an aide, who was a bylaw-man; an official of the manorial courts who enforced the courts orders. 'The figure includes that fellow who was arrested on Saturday as a potential rebel.'

'Ah. Yes, of course.'

'Who was that?' Mullone interjected, suspicion narrowing his face.

The aide, Coilin, was a rakish fellow whose coat seemed far too big for his frame. 'His name is Scurlock, sir, and he was caught trying to sneak into the town.'

'How do you know he's a rebel?'

'When he was apprehended, he was trying to digest a piece of paper, which was found to contain an old address of John Fitzstephen.'

Interesting, Mullone considered. 'Has he talked?' he asked, wondering if Johnson had allowed the use of torture to extract information, but had to be diplomatic in his approach. One wrong word and he would lose the general's co-operation.

Coilin shook his head. 'No, sir. I believe he was initially questioned on the day, but due to the reports of local insurgency, he remains locked away.'

'We need to have a word with him, sir,' McBride said.

'Agreed.'

'Perhaps this Scurlock may know Father Keay, sir?' Mullone turned to Johnson.

The general shrugged, but looked thoughtful.

'May I have your permission to ask him some questions in the morning?'

Mullone would also question him first thing about Black. Was this the man running from him? Mullone could only hope this trail goes somewhere.

'Of course you may, for what little use it may prove,' Johnson agreed and then added, 'however, if we are not attacked.' He sighed and looked at the officers intently, deciding that everything useful had been said. 'Gentlemen, you have your orders for tomorrow, and with any luck, we may be safe in New Ross for another day. Dear God I hope so.'

Mullone and McBride wandered out towards Three Bullet Gate where two regiments flanked the defences with two field guns, and yet more men waited in the trenches. They were quiet, solemn and Mullone stopped to stare up at the night sky where an orange radiance pulsed from the immense black mass of the hill to touch the stars. Campfires: the summit was ringed with so many of them. Mullone could hear voices coming from the glow, laughter, and the sound of a tambourine and a fiddle playing energetically.

'Sounds like they're already celebrating a victory,' Mullone remarked.

'Aye, sir,' McBride agreed. 'I don't blame them.'

Mullone turned to him. 'You'd rather be up there, wouldn't you, Michael?' he asked him without accusing him. He'd let Solomon

58

turn his coat, why not his lieutenant? He stole a glance up to the summit where he was sure he could see figures, like pencil drawings, glare back. His brother had wanted a better life and to be happy, why couldn't McBride do the same too? 'Goddamn conscience,' Mullone muttered.

'Sir?'

Mullone adjusted his neck-tie. 'I almost wish I was up there with them.'

McBride's jaw lolled. 'Sir?'

'They're up there drinking, talking, laughing, sleeping and making love with their sweethearts under the stars, while we're down here quaking in the gutters, waiting for the moment they charge down for our blood.'

'Then, you agree, sir?'

'About what?'

McBride adjusted his spectacles. 'That we're *not* on the winning side.'

Mullone gave his young officer a look of sadness. 'Ah. I never said anything about that, now did I?'

McBride's top teeth worried his bottom lip and he awkwardly shuffled his boots. 'Do you think the prisoner knows anything about Black?'

'I don't know,' Mullone said thoughtfully, 'but we can only hope so. Perhaps the trail will lead us to Black.'

McBride bobbed his head. 'Do you think the garrison is ready?'

Mullone sucked in a breath of night-air. 'As ready as can be,' he said and smiled as a loud lingering laugh from the enemy camp hooted like a crazy owl. 'More so than the poor souls at Prosperous. Some say they deserved it. Their captain was a swine, probably like Torrington, but nothing justifies attacks like that. We're not all like that.' He turned to McBride. 'Go back to your lodgings and wait for me as per your orders. Try to get some sleep.'

'Thank you, sir.'

'Oh, and Michael?'

'Sir?'

'It may not seem it sometimes, but you are on the winning side.'

McBride gave the merest hint of a smile. 'Goodnight, sir,' he said, and walked away into the gloom of the alleys.

Mullone threw a searching look up at the hill. The garrison was ready. The muskets were primed, the guns loaded and the swords sharpened.

The soldiers were ready to fight.

The first thing Mullone knew of the attack was when a musket shot echoed out in the half-light of daybreak. Another musket banged, then another and suddenly hundreds of voices were roaring.

He had to give up his spacious quarters to Lord Mountjoy and had slept for three hours in one of the tiny houses that faced eastwards, overlooking the steep rise of Corbet Hill. He blinked and a shot out of bed as adrenaline coursed through his veins. Buckling his sword belt and risking a quick glance out of the dusty window, he could see thousands of rebels descending the hill in the dawn light, cerise with the blush of summer. It was as though someone had disturbed an ant nest. Bullets hummed and one hit the house with a splintering thud.

'Sergeant Cahill!' Mullone jumped the last flight of stairs to run outside into the street, slipping in horse dung, but managing to remain on his feet. He saw Cahill with a few of the men by a series of barricades cut from timber that some pioneers had lashed together in the night. 'Get the men to their positions,' Mullone said, peering through the gate where a fusillade of musket fire crackled outside the walls.

'Sir,' the sergeant barked and turned to a group of them at the rear. 'Get your arses here! Now! At the double! Jesus, you slow-witted buggers! I can piss faster than that! At the double! Trooper Coveny! You point the muzzle at the enemy, you useless bastard!'

Three riders cantered past them and Mullone saw that the leading horseman was General Johnson and the other two were his aides. Coilin saw Mullone and waved a hand and Mullone dipped his head. The general looked calm and rode out to where the two guns were emplaced by the gates and where the battle raged at the slopes. His horse was a fine steed with a diamond-shaped patch of pristine white against the roan coat and dark mane.

Mullone's dragoons cocked their carbines and slid the barrels over the barricade. A platoon from the Wexford Militia joined them and a white-haired major shook his hand fervently. He spoke with an accent so thick that Mullone had difficulty in understanding him. Mullone just grinned back, and the old major shook his head at the flaccid response, muttered something, and went down the line of his men, checking that bayonets had been fixed.

'He speaks the old language, sir,' Cahill said at Mullone's confusion. 'He's from Forth and Bargy. They speak a different tongue to the rest of us.'

The baronies of Forth and Bargy spoke in a dialect that was of mixed race. The language had grown over centuries from the Viking, Old English and Flemish settlers who had mixed with the Irish and stayed in Wexford.

'What did he say? Was it about me?'

Cahill's face split with a grin. 'You don't want to know, sir.'

Mullone pulled out his fob watch, it was just after five o'clock. Today was Wednesday and the fight to save the town had begun. He wondered if Black would go free if he was killed today? Would someone else catch him? Or would the wretch continue to slaughter? He suddenly became angry and told himself that he would live to

61

see the monster apprehended even if this was the last thing he ever did on this mortal world. His fingers grasped the cross about his neck; Solomon's cross, and he did something that he hadn't done for a long time.

He said the Lord's Prayer.

The two field guns suddenly rumbled to life and Mullone was deafened as roundshot screamed over the forward redcoats to slash gaps in the enemies' front ranks. Mullone saw men punched backwards, pikes and hats snatched away as the two iron balls ploughed into them just like a terrible game of skittles.

'I can hear cattle!' Cahill said over the noise and sure enough a large herd of black cattle were being driven at the defences.

'They tried this at Enniscorthy last week!' Mullone told him. 'The cattle smashed the defences down, sending the garrison into confusion.'

Cahill grinned admiringly. 'Crafty buggers, sir!'

But at Enniscorthy the defenders had not entrenched the ground and the cattle, wide-eyed and stampeding, saw the bayonet-tipped men in the trenches and veered away. The leading redcoats in skirmish order shot at the men who tried to drive them on with staves.

'Fire!' The two battalions began firing by companies and the bullets tore into the rebels as they advanced against the first trench. Many fell, but there were thousands of them coming and the Militia were dangerously threatened with being overrun by the momentum of the advance. Mullone saw an officer flung backwards by a musket ball.

The sound of horses galloping along the cobbles made Johnson turn in his saddle. A score of blue-coated dragoons on chestnuts and greys reached the gates seeking glory with blades glimmering like rods of lightning held high.

'No!' Johnson screamed at them. 'Get back!'

'The damned fools!' Mullone snarled.

But the dragoons were not listening and thundered out to the enemy like avenging angels seeking glory. The horsemen's sabres were excellent for slashing and cutting, but the rebels were armed with ten-foot pikes and Mullone could see death in the long spears. Some were simple spear-like heads, others also had an axe blade like a halberd, but most had a curved blade below the main spearhead which could cut through a horseman's reins and straps, and hook men off their mounts. The horsemen charged straight into the packed lines and were immediately impaled by the block of pikemen. Men fell from their saddles and were soon set upon with clubs, billhooks and hammers. Others were stabbed in their saddles, or pulled down and mercilessly butchered with knives. An officer cleaved in a man's head with his sword, turned to bring the blade up through another enemy's chin to his nose, but a rebel with long black hair swung his pike into the horse's mouth, breaking its teeth. It tossed its head, shrieking, stamped its hooves and blood splattered the lines of pikemen. Whilst the officer struggled to control the beast, another rebel armed with a long handled axe chopped through his right leg at the thigh. He screamed as the limb fell away, and then a pike sliced up into his armpit to end his chance of glory. Within minutes all the dragoons were dead and the rebels advanced with a keening blood-cry.

'Gone! All of them!' Johnson thumped his fist hard into his thigh, face red with ire and frustration. 'A senseless waste of life!'

'A bit like this stinking war,' Corporal Brennan voiced. No one replied, which he took for assent.

Johnson twisted in his saddle to Coilin. 'I don't want any of our horse east of Neville Street or north of the barracks! Relay that message to Captain Buckley. I don't want his Fencibles anywhere in goddamn sight. The cavalry are part of our reserve.'

'Yes, sir.' The aide had to shout over a ripple of gunfire. He plugged an ear with a finger for the sound seemed to reverberate through his body.

'And Coilin, you tell him that if I do, I'll have him on a charge of insubordination.'

Coilin saluted, kicked his heels back and galloped down the street.

The cannons belched flame and the puffs of smoke momentarily blotted out Mullone's view of the battlefield. He heard the blue-coated artillery officer give the order to load with canister and realised that the rebels were closer than he imagined. Johnson then rode up to the gun teams, gave the hill a measured stare, and then ordered them batteries to be pulled back to the first barricades inside the gates. He could not believe his eyes as the rebels ignored the musketry from the walls to push back the forward posts and charge the trenches. The columns were soaking up the bullets like a sponge. Johnson muttered a prayer. It was too late for many of the redcoats. Some of the lucky ones managed to clamber out, but most were trapped. Rebels hacked with swords, clubbed with lumps of wood and speared with pikes.

'Back!' Johnson shouted at the two battalions outside the gates and immediately, his fine horse was shot in the head. The air misted crimson for a brief second. He kicked his heels out of the saddle and jumped free of the dying beast. 'Pull the men back to the secondary positions! Go! Go now!' he ordered, without breaking his nerve and the first Militia battalion shouldered their muskets and the files withdrew quickly like scalded fingers.

The remaining battalion continued firing their volleys towards the trenches as well as the light company men from the Kildare Militia who were firing from rooftops, walls and makeshift firing platforms. Red-coated bodies were stripped of cartridges, boots, shirts and anything the rebels could make use of. A lieutenant, barely seventeen, tried to crawl away and a woman cut his throat with a fish knife. A grenadier wearing a fur cap cried for his mother as men took it in turns to stab him to death as they passed. A group of musket armed rebels opened up on the battalion from the trench works and the bullets tore into the Militia's ranks. Men tumbled, bleeding and dying, their screams were drowned out by the savage salvos of musket, pistol, cannon and the crash of battle.

Johnson's remaining aide, seventeen years old and wearing a brown suit and an old-fashioned tricorn hat, brought up a spare mount. The general lifted himself into the saddle and cantered back past the barricade to assess the defences at the junction of Neville and Michaels' Street and at Bunnion Gate. Colonel Craufurd was in command of the detachments at Main Guard and he had two guns facing down the South Street and east towards the Barracks. If the rebels succeeded in driving in Johnson's defenders at the Three Bullet Gate, he reckoned that they would be stopped at Main Guard. *They would have to be*, he said to himself, for it was the heart of the town and if the heart was taken, then New Ross was dead.

The last battalion complete with the Colours filed in through the gate in reasonable order, but at the last moment the men's courage broke and they began to scatter in droves.

'Jesus!' Cahill shook his head in disgust at the redcoats who bolted past the barricades despite the best efforts of the officers and NCO's who tried to inculcate order. They could go nowhere else because Johnson had strategically blocked various roads throughout the town with stone, timber and wagons and would funnel any attacks in one direction from the gates to where the armed detachments waited.

The gun teams had finished pulling back the two cannon with ropes as the Militia bolted and the captain, a barrel-chested man with bow legs, ordered the iron killers to be double-shotted with canister. Both muzzles pointed at the gates and, if they could be loaded in time, would obliterate the assault in an explosion of flame and smoke.

The light company skirmishers on the walls and roofs gradually moved away from the gates for fear of being hit from behind. The air was thick with smoke as they fired at the enemy on the plain.

'Here they come!' one of the redcoats shouted from his position on the wall next to the gate. Mullone took a deep breath, bracing himself like a man striding into a storm. His sword was drawn, but he kept thinking of sheathing it. He was a soldier, but it did not feel right to fight men; Irish men, who were not wearing military uniforms. It was a rare and terrible thing to fight your own people. How had it come to this? Then, he found that he had forgotten to bring his helmet from the billet and thought that it was unlucky. For a heartbeat, he considered that he would die unless he retrieved it, but then ridiculed himself for that notion.

'I'll shoot the first bastard that shows his face!' Trooper Coveny boasted loudly, fiddling with the trigger guard that hung loose because the screw was lost. 'I'll send the croppie to an early grave.'

'You couldn't hit a target through an open window, Coveny,' Cahill replied, 'so still your bullshit!' The dragoons laughed at the swollen-eyed trooper.

Mullone knew that Coveny's flippant remark was because of nerves. The sound of the rebel army approaching, the great seething mass of men bristling with weapons could put ice-cold fear in a man or turn his bowels to water.

Behind them a mounted Militia officer was trying to control his horse. Its eyes were bulging wide and wet nostrils flared black. It snorted loudly and whinnied. 'There, there. Calm yourself, Rascal,' the officer said soothingly. 'It'll soon be over, boy. There, there.'

'Ready yourselves!' Mullone heard himself say, which was strange, he thought, for he knew his men were prepared.

A great cry came from beyond the walls that were punctuated by musket blasts and Mullone readied himself for the guns to leap into action. Mullone felt a tremor. The ground shook and then the first rebels poured through the gates like an oncoming tide. Mullone saw the leading man; both hands gripping a green banner, face contorted with zeal. The flag had a white cross in the centre of the green field and the initials JF below it. John Fitzstephen. Then, there were more men behind him, tens, then scores. Pike heads glittered. And then time seemed to slow.

The guns erupted barely twenty feet from them.

Later on, Mullone would remember the great streaks of flame leap from the muzzles to lick the air and all of the charging rebels were shredded and riven in one terrible, sweeping instant. Balls ricocheted on stone and great chunks were gouged out by the bullets. Blood sprayed on the walls as far back as the arched gateway, limbs were shorn off, and Mullone watched in horror as a bloodied head tumbled down the sloped street towards the barricade.

'Jesus sweet suffering Christ!' Cahill gawped at the carnage as the echo of the big guns resonated like a giant's beating heart.

Trooper O'Shea bent to one side and vomited at the sight of the twitching, bleeding and unrecognisable lumps that had once been human beings. A man staggered with both arms missing. A rebel buckled to his knees, holding his own entrails. Another crawled back to the gate with a shattered legs spurting blood. The stench of burnt flesh and the iron tang of blood hung ripe and nauseating in the oppressive air.

One of the low wooden cabins by the wall was aflame. A blast of musketry outside the walls rattled against the stonework and a redcoat toppled backwards with a gasp onto the roof.

'Here they come again! Ready your firelocks! Do not waste a shot!' Johnson shouted in a steady voice as the gateway became thick with more enemies. He took a deep breath.

'God forgive us,' Corporal Brennan said.

'Liberty or death!' A rebel, armed with a blood-stained pitchfork, shouted over-and-over.

'Fire!' Johnson yelled and muskets and carbines crashed from the barricades, doors, windows and roof tops. Whole lines of the attackers were jerked back. The pitch-fork wielding rebel went down, his blood thick on the cobblestones. Another tripped on a body and was shot in the mouth as he scrambled to get up. One attacker holding a banner with one hand burst forward and brought out a large horse pistol to shoot dead a gunner. The redcoats let loose another volley and more rebels fell from the bullets. The rear rebel ranks were pushing the front forward and one man shot in the thigh fell backwards and was slowly crushed by the sheer weight of attackers.

'Load!' Johnson wanted the men to have one last volley before the insurgents reached them en masse.

The wounded soldier on the roof began to scream as the flames fanned across the wood.

Cahill tracked a man holding one of the flags and put a bullet in his brain. The rebels able to bring their captured muskets from the dead Militia to bear began to fire at the barricades. A bullet splinted the wood next to Mullone's hand.

'Bayonets!' Johnson ordered once the guns were loaded. 'Gunners fall back!' He waved at the teams to move behind the barricades. 'Let the rebels dash themselves on our cold blades!'

The United men reached the fleeing gunners and those that could not get away were killed where they stood. Then scrambled to the barricades with a roar of triumph where steel waited for them.

'Fire!' Johnson waved his sword down in one snapping arc.

Muskets coughed and the first ranks of the enemy were thrown back in a maelstrom of lead and blood. No sooner as the foul-smelling powder smoke cleared, the next ranks came forth. The clamour of their voices was tumultuous like many waves breaking upon a rocky shore.

'Swords!' Mullone shouted and the dragoons slung their used carbines across their backs and withdrew their 1796 issue cavalry sabres. They were well oiled, so that they slid free with barely a sound.

'Now kill them!' Johnson screamed savagely. 'Death to traitors!'

'Let's break some skulls!' Cahill shouted as he swept aside two pikes with his sword. He chopped down and the cavalry sword cleaved down through an opponent's head as thought it were a hen's egg. Brain glistened and spilt like runny yolk. The other assailant reacted quicker, bringing out a broad-bladed knife, teeth bared in a grimace of pure hatred. He was dressed in dirty peasant smocks, his body thin and face pitted, but fury and zeal had transformed him into a formidable foe. He swept the blade at Cahill; a series of arcing swipes, forcing the sergeant back as another man with hooded eyes that were wide in terror and excitement, came at him with a rusted cutlass. The sergeant stayed out of their reach, but stepping ever backwards, he suddenly brought his sword forward and the blade flashed through the peasant's wrist, severing the hand that still gripped the knife. He staggered and then the sword struck again, this time cleaving his face in two. The second man brushed past his compatriot and thrust his old sword at Cahill's chest, hoping that one quick, hard blow would work. Except that the sergeant had seen the attack in his enlarged eyes and flicked his sword up, parrying the attack, to scythe across the man's throat. He sunk to his knees, blood gurgling and hands clasping at the hideous wound.

'Jesus, this one stinks like a dead hog left out in the rain,' Cahill said, giving the dying man a kick.

The defenders fought with ferocity, stabbing and cutting with a vicious frenzy. It was a street fight; a gutter brawl where men fought like animals for the need to survive. Mullone saw a tall man with black hair in a long green coat working his way towards the redcoats from the gateway, pushing the men forward and rallying the gaps where men's courage failed. He was a brave man and it was at that moment that a rider from the garrison galloped to the barricade, vaulted it clear and urged his mount towards him. The horse ploughed through the mass of rebels, knocking them back, but the red-coated officer had not drawn his sword. It was Lord Mountjoy. Mullone could hear him trying to persuade them to surrender peacefully. He appealed to them with arms outstretched, he spoke of being kin, but they would not listen to him and he was pulled from his horse and dragged to the gateway where a pike ran through his chest to touch the stonework behind. Blood pumped from his open mouth as he died.

'Major!' Johnson called down to Mullone as a surge of Militiamen swelled the bayoneted ranks. 'We can hold them here. Take your men to Colonel Craufurd. Assist him at Main Guard!'

'Yes, sir,' Mullone replied. He twisted to his men. 'Follow me!' The dragoons broke from combat to follow him back down the street where more Militia were pressing forward with bayonets and charged muskets.

They ran down an abandoned Neville Street and turned left into Marys Street which was very steep. A man, trying to shelter from the assault, ran into an alley seeking solace. Mullone wasn't sure if he was a redcoat or not. Their boots echoed loudly as they reached the cobbled crossroads at Main Guard, which were strong with defenders.

'You bring orders?' Craufurd called, resplendent in his uniform, as several Colours rippled in the gentle breeze behind him. Men stared at them wondering what dismounted cavalry were doing here.

'No, sir,' Mullone said. 'General Johnson is holding Three Bullet Gate. He ordered me to assist you.'

'Assist? Well, find a position and try not to get in anyone's way,' he said irritably.

'Yes, sir.'

Suddenly, the two guns facing South Street roared and Craufurd immediately went to investigate their discharge. Mullone followed.

'I spotted movement down by the gardens, sir,' said the gun team captain.

Craufurd rounded on him. 'How do you know they weren't ours?'

The captain ran a powder-smeared hand across his forehead, dislodging sweat-matted hair that hung loose from his hat. 'I saw pikes, sir. Lots of them.'

Craufurd frowned. 'They must have somehow breached the Priory Gate.'

Mullone scanned the cobbled street. How in Christ's name had they achieved that? He heard shouts and men yelling and became all too clear that the rebels had found a weakness and were already converging to the towns heart. 'They must have, sir,' Mullone told him. 'No rebel had got past the defences at Three Bullet Gate.'

'I had shored it up tight with timber and stone,' Craufurd said, in a disgruntled tone. 'Captain O'Dwyer and his men should have sent word of any attack. I fear the worst.' A bullet snicked the wall beside him, fired from the captured gate. He returned to the defences stretched across the road where the Glengarry Fencibles held them. 'Wait until I give you the command to fire!' his voice boomed at the Highlanders who wore kilts, yellow-faced jackets and bonnets without the black ostrich feathers that usually embellished such headgear. 'Do not fire until I give you the word! Fellow men of Scotland, you will wait for my command!' The small colonel repeated his order until his voice was hoarse with the strain.

He knew full well that Militia and Fencible battalions were not as disciplined as the regular line troops and he did not want them to waste a volley. One error of judgment and the defence would be thrown into tatters. Craufurd would wait until the insurgents were at least thirty yards from the barricades and then, and only then, he would give the command to fire. And then they appeared at the slight bend in the road, stalking and moving cautiously. They could see the blockaded street. They knew muskets waited for them and yet, they still approached.

'Load!' Mullone yelled at his dragoons.

The rebel commanders were dressed in their Sunday best, and their hats were furnished with green plumes and white hat bands. Around their waists, or slung over shoulders, were green sashes and on their breasts, green badges showed the golden harp. The rest were dressed in their work clothes, or peasant smocks adorned with green bushy twigs in their flowerpot shaped hats. Some even wore Tarleton helmets, grenadier caps and bicorns plundered from bodies. The lucky ones carried muskets.

'*Erin Go Bragh*!' the rebels shouted. Ireland forever.

'Liberty or death!'

And then they came at the defences; fearless and with absolute conviction for their cause. They sprinted and they ran. Mullone saw that they were armed with all manner of pike, sword, knife, club and axe. He could also see two priests, one was armed with a mace and the other carried a blunderbuss. Neither of them were De Marin. A pair of hands somewhere in the mass held up a large wooden cross. Mullone unconsciously touched the cross at his neck hoping that his prayers were answered too.

A rebel, his mouth torn wide in a battle cry, waved his sword. 'Kill them all!'

Craufurd was calm. 'Present! Fire!'

Two hundred and fifty muskets and carbines exploded and it seemed to Mullone that the rebels were suddenly jerked back by invisible ropes, and then were completely obscured by a bank of filthy smoke.

Ramrods frantically scraped down the barrels as the Highlanders and dragoons reloaded. The rebels jumped their fallen and immediately the long-reaching pikes thrust and stabbed at the redcoats. But Craufurd had piled so much on the barricades that the rebels found even their ten and twelve foot pikes were too cumbersome here. Men kicked at the obstacles and pulled at the great stones, broken cart wheels, carriages, boxes and barrels. Hands and arms bled from crude *chevaux de frise* as they tore at the barricade like frenzied animals. A rebel armed with a musket rammed it between a gap, pulled the trigger and a Scotsman fell back with a ball through an eye. Mullone knocked a pike back with his sword and then saw that the musket-armed rebel was a woman. She was dressed in a green satin dress and was startlingly beautiful. Their eyes met; and he could do nothing but stare at her. Then, the soldiers brought muskets to their shoulders and through the openings and suddenly, Mullone's vision was fogged with gritty smoke. A bullet smacked against the iron hoops of a barrel and he instinctively ducked. When he looked up, the woman was gone, leaving him to wonder if she had died from the volley, or was safely aside.

'Fire!'

Mullone's men knelt with loaded carbines and poured bullets at point-blank range into the innumerable enemy. 'Fire!' Cahill was keening with battle-joy. 'Keep firing, you bastards! Send them to Hell!'

'Hold the Colours!' An officer shouted as a rock hit the sixteen-year-old ensign carrying it. A sergeant helped up the bleeding junior officer and the Union Flag was raised high again.

A rebel threw his pike like a javelin and the weapon lodged between the spokes of an upturned cart. A woman wearing a green shawl hacked at the barricade with a set of spurs, a young man who had never seen a pike two weeks ago, now lay next to her with blood-roses blooming on his frayed white shirt. Another was coiled like a foetus from the bullet wound to his groin.

Craufurd waved his sword. 'Highlanders fire! Drive the blackguards back!'

'No quarter for the king's dogs!' A rebel countered.

Those Scotsmen who could reload, as most were defending the barricades with bayonets, did so and the steel ramrods twirled in the air so that they skimmed their knuckles on the long blades. A light company soldier, drunk before the fight had started, mistakenly left his ramrod in the barrel. He pulled the trigger and it shot out to skewer an attacker in the face. The soldier laughed like a crazed man. Ball after musket ball ripped into the rebel horde that pushed and fought against the musket-tipped blockade. The dead were piling up and the living were choking in the throat-drying acrid air.

'They'll never get through these tough bastards, sir!' Cahill shouted, raising his helmet and dragging an arm across his face, smearing grime and sweat. 'They can't get over their own dead!'

Suddenly, from Michaels Lane, Mullone saw a block of advancing shadows and, for a second, he could not believe his eyes. Panic bubbled in the back of his throat.

'Look out! Get down!' he screamed and managed to the sergeant down as a protracted volley slammed into the defenders. Fifteen dragoons and Highlanders were killed by the musket armed rebels.

'Christ! Watch them!' Craufurd exclaimed, stunned that the enemy had penetrated this far into the town. 'Load! Running fire!' he added to allow the men to fire at will.

Cahill bent down to one of the dragoons, closing his lifeless eyes. One of them was swollen and bruised blue-black.

Mullone looked up from Trooper Coveny. 'They must have broken into the barracks, and stolen the arms and shot,' he said, staring at the sixty-odd armed rebels.

Craufurd brought his reserves to fight off the new attackers and Mullone saw a flicker of worry cross his face.

'I'll go back and check Main Guard, sir,' he said, understanding the situation. There was a narrow street that led from the barracks to the cross junction and the Scotsman was wondering if the enemy had got behind them, thus cutting them off.

'Hurry! And report back to me immediately!' Craufurd said, before turning back to supervise the men where one Highlander screamed pitifully as a pike had sliced open his belly. Another coughed up blood. 'Push them back!' he crowed at the redcoats. 'Give them the steel! Go on! Push them back all the way! They won't break us!'

Mullone remembered from the officer's mess that Craufurd had stubbornly refused the idea of withdrawing from New Ross, or the possibility of surrendering. He considered that Craufurd was like Moore, both Scottish, confident and experienced, but Moore would always consider and respect other men's opinions whilst Craufurd could be obstinate and tough to deal with. But now here in the fight for survival, Craufurd could be relied on to manage the garrison and lead the troops. There was no one better.

Mullone sucked in a sulphurous breath that stung his throat. 'Lord Lovell's Dragoons! To me! To me!' His voice snapped sharp and crisp above the din. The dragoons, their faces sooty with powder, hotfooted to the junction. A terrified lieutenant wearing an ill-fitting coat met them near the gaol. It was deserted.

'Someone sprang the prisoners in the night, sir,' he said, jerking a thumb at the stone building. 'They're all gone.'

Mullone looked at Cahill. Scurlock, the man he planned to question, had vanished. It all seemed too convenient.

'Did anyone see who was responsible?' Mullone asked, chest heaving.

'No, sir.'

'It's a gaol!' Mullone threw up his hands. 'It's supposed to be guarded! Where were the guards?'

The lieutenant looked as though he was about to break down. 'I don't know, sir. I'm not the gaoler.'

'Where is he?'

'If he had any sense, he'd be on the way to Waterford by now, sir.'

'Here they come!' shouted a voice from the Court House and Mullone pushed past the lieutenant to see two long columns of rebels coming straight at them; one smaller group from the barracks and the other worryingly from Neville Street from the direction of Three Bullet Gate.

'The buggers have probably come from the two western gates,' Cahill suggested, as he finished loading his carbine. 'I doubt that they've beaten the general.'

A bearded priest led the smaller column and Mullone stared at the face, recognising the man instantly. The hair was cut short and the beard was full, and the last time he had seen this man, he had been dressed in the uniform of the French *Légion Irlandaise*. At his hip hung an expensive sabre, sheathed in a simple cloth covered scabbard.

'De Marin!' Mullone hollered, unsheathing his sword.

The Frenchman looked utterly astonished for a second, withdrew his sabre and then offered his nemesis a huge grin, like those reserved for old acquaintances meeting after being apart for some time. He hauled free his sword, pointing it like a steel finger at Mullone, and then moved aside. Mullone saw a cannon muzzle. A man wearing a red Phrygian cap waved a black flag emblazoned with the mocking words stitched in white 'God Damn The King'.

'Give this to your poxed king!' A gunner shouted.

Mullone pulled down Cahill as the cannon roared and belched fiery smoke. The iron ball smashed into the barricade, ploughing straight through it to cut a man in half, disembowel another, and showered a dozen men with wicked debris. A private staggered back with a foot long splinter sticking out of his chest.

Mullone was dazed. He shook his head and saw that a shard of wood from a carriage wheel was sticking in his right boot-top. He pulled it out and groaned. He peeled back the leather to see that his knee was gashed open. A splinter of jagged wood was sticking out of his flesh and he tugged it free, feeling the wood scrape bone.

'That's twice now, sir!' Cahill rasped, as he helped Mullone to his feet. 'I hope to God you don't want this paid back in whiskey?'

Mullone took of his white necktie and tied it around the wound. He pressed his foot down and despite the pain, found that he could at least stand.

'De Marin's here!' he uttered and turned to see if the Frenchman was in sight, but could not see him in the great press of men.

Cahill looked incredulous. 'That bastard?'

The rebels were clawing at the barricades. A loose volley of musketry smashed into the redcoats killing three men and wounding a half-dozen more. A private, arm shattered by a musket ball, tried to bayonet a rebel who was clambering over the barricade, but a woman wearing a green bonnet jumped on him and swung a small hatchet into his forehead. Dark gore sprayed up into her face, but she was screaming in Gaelic and hacking wildly as the man twitched and died beneath her. A grenadier corporal of the Londonderry Militia shoved a man back, kicked the legs from under another and bayoneted both men with such force that both times the steel went through cloth and flesh to pierce the stone cobbles underneath.

'*Erin Go Bragh*!' De Marin shouted from somewhere in the throng and immediately tens of voices cried out the same chant.

Swords lunged and sliced, crossed and scraped, bayonets stabbed and pikes speared. The rebel dead were making their own barricades. A dog tugged intestines from a corpse. A little girl ran over to fallen redcoats and cut off their cartridge boxes with a knife and returned them to where the armed rebels were waiting in lines, desperate for ammunition.

'Death to the king's men!'

De Marin cut one man down and then speared the young terrified Militia lieutenant through the heart as he charged him. 'Fire!' he shouted while he was still killing the officer. The rebel lines flamed brightly, bullets hummed and buzzed and redcoats tumbled backwards onto the cobbles, or collapsed at the blockades. A rebel managed to dart up the barricade and aimed his blunderbuss. One of Mullone's dragoons saw him and put a carbine ball between his ribs. The dying rebel still managed to pull the trigger as two redcoats climbed up to stop him. They were instantly torn apart by the mixture of lead balls, nails and stones that exploded from the weapons' wide muzzle. Mullone was splattered by droplets of human debris.

Men kicked at the barricades, others dropped their weapons to heave aside the stones, the wagons and cut trees, all the time the redcoats shot at them and gouged with bayonets. Pike heads pricked the air in staccato thrusts. A big man wielding a hammer made a gap and the rebels poured through it.

'Seán!' Mullone yelled, pointing his sword at the threat. He shouldered a man wearing a black shirt to the ground, and kicked him between the legs when he tried to get up. A man wearing a top hat brought down a lump of timber in the hope of crushing his head, but Mullone leapt aside and punched his sword arm forward to break the man's nose. Another rebel armed with a scythe tried to slice Mullone across the belly, but he managed to parry it, grunting with the impact. The blades met, clashed and the shock jolted Mullone's fingers, palm and wrist. Gripping his sword in two hands, he drove both blades to the ground.

'You pup!' The man snarled and Mullone could smell the foul stench of decay wafting from his gums. The muscles in his arms looked like knotted rope. 'I've killed plenty of you king's men today with this. I'll tear out your stinking guts.'

Mullone, teeth clenched, found he could not hold his grip for long because the man was evidently stronger. He slapped Mullone away with a muscled arm, thundered forward and then Cahill shot him plumb in the chest.

'Are you all right, sir?'

'Yes,' Mullone clutched the sergeant's forearm as a thank you.

'So we're even then?' Cahill gave a wry, lop-sided grin.

Mullone saw that the makeshift bandage was soaked through with blood. 'We need support,' he said, knowing that they would be soon overrun. And if Mullone lost here, then Craufurd and his defenders would be flooded with attackers and massacred. He saw movement to his right. A boy snuck through gaps in the barricade and dodged through legs to reach him. The boy was not even ten years old, but was armed with a sharp iron rod and suddenly brought it towards Mullone who easily parried the small attacks with his sword.

'Go back home, boy,' he said, flicking the rod away.

The boy slashed wildly. Cahill cackled with laughter which seemed to incense him even more.

'Go home!' Mullone said and slapped the back of the boy's head with the flat-side of the sword. The boy cursed him before running to disappear behind one of the houses where a Militia drummer was slumped against a wall, drunk and oblivious to the fighting. Somewhere a man spilled the contents of his stomach and then made a gurgling sound.

The rebels, exhilarated by the victory, surged towards the larger group who were trying to hold Main Guard. The clash of steel on steel and steel on wood was louder than any musketry, for few men had time to load their muskets, and so used their blades, or heavy stocks of their guns instead of powder and ball.

Craufurd had brought back the Highlanders from South Street. 'There's no hope in holding them back,' he said disappointedly, as the files of redcoats extricated themselves from the killing field. Their faces were streaked with gunpowder and sweat. 'We'll hold them here and then fall back to the secondary position at the North Gate, if we need to.'

'What about the bridge, sir?' Mullone asked and ducked as the cannon fired again and its roundshot went high to smack into the corner of one of the houses. Stone and mortar tumbled onto the roadside.

'Would you see how they're faring, Major?' Craufurd asked. 'We must hold it at all costs!'

'I understand, sir,' Mullone nodded, as Cahill closed the lids of a dead trooper, a ragged mess where the lower part of his face had once been.

The remaining troopers ran to the quay, where the streets were narrow and twisting, until they came to the actual harbour that stank of fetid water and shit. Mullone half-limped and gritted his teeth at the agony of his exertion.

The bridge was full of townsfolk hurriedly retreating to Rosbercon. There were scores of mounted men and several canvass covered wagons too. He looked around to see if McBride was at his position near the North Gate but, pushing past scores of people and horses, he could not see him or their mounts. Mullone had posted McBride with six men near the abbey and all the mounts. Gulls cried over the buildings, smoke from several house fires to the south rose high above the harbour to drift across the Barrow. Where was McBride? Or the six troopers?

'Perhaps he's gone over the bridge, sir?' Cahill suggested, seeing the major's expression.

Mullone did not know. It wasn't like the lieutenant to disobey him. He gave the order for the men to load their carbines. There were six men missing, Cahill gave him the names. A splintering crash of musketry from the direction of South Street followed by a woman screaming caused Mullone to investigate it. If the rebels succeeded in breaking the defences here, the quay would be lost along with the bridge. A surge of panicking folk swept through the dragoons.

Mullone battered one man away and Cahill punched a man who tried to grab his carbine. The major hobbled around the corner to see a group of redcoats fighting with insurgents at the top of the road. The Militia were beaten down and the enemy swarmed over the bodies.

'In here!' a man shouted and Mullone looked up at the buildings, searching for the caller. A grey-haired man waved at them from one of the houses down the road. 'Get inside, you dullards!' he shouted as a large group of rebels converged on the road. They were surrounded.

'Jesus, you can't be serious, sir?' Cahill asked Mullone.

'Have you a better idea?'

'Once the mob knows we're inside, they'll tear down every wall to get to us. We'll be trapped like eels in a basket. It's a stupid idea. It's like taking a whore to meet your mother.'

This was not the time for indecision.

'Inside!' Mullone ignored Cahill and pushed the men towards the doorway. A young man wearing a pale shirt and an ammunition belt let them in. The dragoons fired at the two groups and a handful of rebels went down. A pistol shot killed one of Mullone's troopers as he attempted to reload and another was struck in the face with a rock.

'O'Shea! Get inside, you whoreson!' Cahill pushed the bleeding trooper and a rebel armed with an old broadsword ran up to the sergeant and stabbed it through his thigh. Cahill hissed through gritted teeth and thumped the stock of his carbine into the man's jaw, breaking it with a sickening crack. Another, sliced down with an axe, but the sergeant twisted nimbly aside despite the sword still stuck firm in his flesh, and knocked the rebel to the floor. Cahill then rammed the carbine's muzzle into his open mouth and pulled the trigger. It exploded and the back of the man's head seemed to vanish in a spray of bloody gristle that fanned the cobbles.

'Get him in!' Mullone ordered and two troopers grabbed Cahill inside. Hands clasped the door shut, but a sudden pressure was forcing it open.

'Jesus!' said O'Shea, rivulets of blood streaming down his ragged cheek, as he tried to help close the door. 'They're going to break it down!' He had to shout over the pounding, cursing and kicking.

Mullone took a lungful of sulphurous breath. 'Open it!' he said, bringing his sword to bear. 'Ready your blades!'

The trooper stared at him and then obeyed. The door swung open and three rebels tumbled inwards onto the stone floor and were immediately butchered with blades. Mullone charged over the dying men with a roar. An astonished rebel, sword outwards, found himself facing the major's own blade which skewered forward so savagely that the tip struck the far wall after it had gone clean through his body. Mullone withdrew it, and muskets banged to send two more rebels backwards, turning the alley slippery with blood. A carbine fired from the alley and the bullet struck Mullone's scabbard to ricochet with a hum. A rebel whose pike blade was dark with congealed blood, rammed it at Mullone, who twirled himself clear, and grappled the shaft to pull the man forward, hammering the sword hilt into his eyes.

A giant of a man whose face was all beard tried to pulverise Mullone with a long-handled hammer. 'I'll break you apart like old bones in a grave.'

Mullone saw the threat, ducked and the big iron head whipped through the air to smash into the wall, gouging a crater as though a twelve-pounder had hit it. He twisted away as the rebel swung the hammer with enough force to knock over an ox. Mullone stabbed his sword into the man's flank and he stumbled backwards with a dark stain appearing on his shirt. It must have hurt, but the man was frenzied and refused to die. The hammer swung again and Mullone's sword flashed in the blood-reeking alley to send three fingers spinning onto the ground. The man spluttered and Mullone opened up his chest, thrust the hilt to jar against bone, and he was down on his knees. Behind the dying giant, more rebels appeared and Mullone saw jaws set and faces sour with hatred.

Red arms seized Mullone, dragging him back inside the house where the door slammed and was bolted shut by a young man with two pistols tucked in his belt. Two more civilians put up four lengths of timber and quickly struck them across the door with long nails as it rattled and thudded from the enemy outside.

'You're dead men! All of you!' A voice threatened from the other side of the door.

'Well, that was closer than I'd hoped,' Cahill wheezed, trying to stem the flow of blood with his ragged sash after he had pulled the reddened blade free. A chair was fetched and strips of pale cloth were tied around the wound. 'Watch that door!'

The house was owned by the harbour-master and it was he that had accosted them from upstairs. He was called Sawbridge and walked with a wooden leg caused by a boating accident when he was sixteen. He proudly showed off his two sons, his brother and three friends who had taken shelter and had hitherto killed and wounded a score of rebels from the windows upstairs. Sawbridge kindly shared what little food they had, as his wife cleaned Cahill's wound with bandages and boiled water.

Shapes moved outside along the lanes and alleys. The rebels were lighting thatched roofs with pike heads tied with flaming rags. Mullone could hear men howling and screaming like feral beasts down the streets and alleys in search of more butchery, but it seemed they were left alone. The injured coughed and groaned. Sawbridge wanted to kill as many rebels that appeared, but Mullone told him to save his powder in case the house was attacked again and he reluctantly agreed.

They had survived for now, but Mullone wondered how long they must stay here and endure as the guns hammered on, their discharge ringing the town with orange-flame and smoke.

General Johnson had ridden down to survey the attacks at Main Guard and arrived no sooner than to see the redcoats be pushed back to the North Gate. He kicked his spurs back to see the bridge full of frightened townsfolk and rattled Militia. The rebels had now taken the quay and there was no hope of rallying the men here, so he joined the swarm of people in the hope of assembling them at Rosbercon, waving his sword, the reflected fires dancing at its tip like molten silver. But for now it was over. The rebels were victorious. They had beaten the king's soldiers.

New Ross had fallen.

It was eight o'clock.

Mullone waited in the house, hearing the rebels outside, but there were so much battle smoke that he could not see anything, even when he peered out of the window. *It was like London fog*, he reflected. He could hear the constant sound of musketry to the east and north and reckoned that the rebels had not completely taken the town. Even the group outside had given up and dispersed. Then, at noon as the sun burned from above, the shouting became a murmur of voices, the musketry a dull ragged tearing sound, and the caustic smoke thinned to leave the town washed in destruction.

The rebels were exhausted. The cauldron of blood-letting had boiled over and the flames had been doused. It was then that

Johnson rallied the troops who stormed back across the bridge and through the North gate, and the tired rebels could not hope to turn aside the counter-attack. A great deal had fallen where they stood from exhaustion and some had broken into cellars and quenched their thirst with hidden kegs of ale and whiskey. The fight had gone from them.

The redcoats advanced with a savagery that the general could not control, for the men wanted revenge, and would not stop until the last of the rebels were dead. The Dublin Militia, hearing that their commander Lord Mountjoy had been killed, cut bloody swathes through the narrow streets in revenge. A group of redcoats found a house where wounded and exhausted rebels had taken shelter and they shot and bayoneted them all without mercy.

'When we've retaken the town, we go after Black,' Mullone said loud enough for all the men to hear. 'That is our mission. It still stands.'

'Right, sir,' Cahill said and attempted to stand, but Mullone eased him back in the chair where his foot rested on a keg. Sweat beaded the sergeant's pale face and his eyes were red-rimmed.

'No, Seán,' Mullone shook his head. 'Time for you to rest. Same goes for the other four.' He glanced at O'Shea's face, swollen with a great weal under an eye. 'The injured stay here. Mister and Mrs Sawbridge will take care of you.'

Cahill reluctantly agreed and Mullone shook his hand. 'Go break some skulls, sir.'

'You need to heal up before you can make a journey so stay put. What about your wife?'

'She can take care of herself, sir,' Cahill said dismissively with a grin. 'She's got a musket and a fowling piece and a temper to match. The Croppies won't go near her, if they know what's good for them.'

Mullone edged to the door, wound throbbing. He cast a look back at his bandy-legged friend. 'Take care of yourself, Seán. I'll come back.'

'Make sure you do, sir,' Cahill saluted him.

'And you still owe me,' Mullone said, giving his friend a grin.

The major led his remaining dragoons out into the streets where homes smouldered red, wounded crawled and blood dripped; the signs of tragedy. There were bodies everywhere, stiff limbed, punctured with musket balls or laid open by steel. They lay like seeds tossed to the wind. Black smoke was roiling up to the heavens. A troop of Scottish Fencibles galloped past, eager to hunt down the insurgents, shifting tendrils of the pungent smoke that stung Mullone's eyes. He blinked the tears away. Symbols of the harp with an absent crown were etched into walls, painted on doors and chalked on floors. Groups of redcoats drifted away to look for plunder and drink. The liquor shops had been destroyed to protect the men from temptation, but it didn't stop them from ransacking what was left. The lucky ones rolled out hidden casks of port, guzzled spirits and carried away joints of ham and sacks of oats. A civilian tried to stop a Militiaman from looting his house and was shot dead. A companion, laughing at the murder, was urinating against the broken down door. A powder-stained officer, with a tethered mule flanked by two armed confederates, tied more stolen goods onto the beasts back before leaving in search for more plunder.

Mullone went back towards the abbey where he found Black-Eyed Brennan looking after the horses. *Tintreach* whickered a greeting and Mullone patted its face with affection. The numerous fires made the air so hot that it began to sear their throats.

'Have we won, sir?' Brennan enquired.

A team of artillerymen, led by a sergeant with a syphilitic mouth, were pulling recaptured guns with ropes, straining hard with the effort. The cannons were splattered with streaks of dark gore.

'I'm not sure to be honest,' Mullone replied with a shrug. The world as he knew it had been flipped on its heels and now everything that he knew had changed. 'Where's Lieutenant McBride?'

'I don't know, sir,' the corporal looked pained. 'He went in the night. Me and the boys stayed here like you ordered us to, but we had to take cover in one of the houses.' A group of redcoats were shooting pigs that had broken free of their pens and began butchering their corpses for the cooking fires. More were running past laughing madly and crowing at the jugs of wine, shirts, pipes, shoes and silver plate that mirrored the dull-orange fires in their grasp.

'Boys, I've been fishing!' one of them shouted. 'Care to see my catch?' Raucous laughter echoed down the blood-slick road.

Mullone rubbed his tired face and fingered the tight bandage around his knee that Sawbridge had insisted on replacing. He saw several canvasses scattered on the cobbles, all of them riddled with musket ball marks. The paintings had been cut from frames and the portraits used for target practice.

'I don't have the time to look for the lieutenant, so we gather our equipment and find Colonel Black.'

Tintreach would ride like the wind and Mullone vowed that he would not give up searching for Black and De Marin until Judgement Day.

'You're going after Black?' called a voice and Mullone spun round to see a heavyset man with a boy approach him from the abbey. The man was armed with a blunderbuss and an axe was tucked in his belt.

'Who are you?'

'My names Pádraig Scurlock, and I'm the brother of the man they imprisoned here. This is his son, Dónall.'

'I'm not after your brother, or his son,' Mullone said, 'but I hear Black is after him in connection with a killing up in Oldbridge. Do you know anything about that?'

Scurlock bobbed his head curtly. 'My brother and his boy are the only survivors from *Uaimh Tyrell*. You heard about that?'

'What Irishman hasn't?'

'He came after my brother, because he and some United men killed a couple of his dragoons during a raid on a farmstead. Nothing else. Don't believe anything else you hear. Black's men were about to murder the people when my brother stopped them. I guess Black wants revenge.'

'Was this near Oldbridge?'

'Yes,' Scurlock replied cautiously. 'How do you know that?'

'Through lines of enquiry, my dear fellow. Do you know where I can find your brother?' Scurlock shook his head. 'I told you I'm not after him,' Mullone reiterated. 'I'm only after Black. I want that bastard stopped.'

Scurlock watched his nephew for a second before answering. 'Clanfield Manor. South of Enniscorthy. You'll find him there.'

The name rang a bell. 'Is that in any relation to Sir Edward Clanfield?'

'Aye, it's his home,' Scurlock sighed. 'My brother says the United men want him for something. I don't know what for. It's none my business.'

Mullone climbed up into his saddle. 'Why are you telling me this?'

Scurlock looked at the Barrow, the mass of civilians and redcoats and to the sails of boats returning from across the water. 'Because I'm loyal,' he said simply.

Mullone thanked him and the dragoons rode out of the burning town.

They followed the roads north always keeping west of the retreating hordes of insurgents that fled the fires and billowing chaotic smoke over the towers and spires of New Ross. The sky was splashed orange and soon the warm evening turned to night and, as they came within five miles of Enniscorthy, the wide road was clogged with the fractured mass of fleeing rebels. They could not hope to reach the town, or find Sir Edward's manor in the ruddy glow of the sunset, so Mullone took them back to a tiny village they had passed to wait until dawn's first chink of light.

Mullone left sentinels to guard the road and slept an uneasy sleep in a farmer's tumbledown house. The villagers had offered his troopers their barns, byres and spare rooms that smelt of dust, dry fodder and the tang of animal dung. Mullone settled down to sleep in a tiny room laced with spider webs that shivered slightly from a breeze that cut through the rot beneath the windowsill. Shafts of light poured in from holes in the thatch and walls, where tiny motes danced. The farmer and his wife slept next door and both snored and grunted deafeningly.

Despite this, Mullone soon drifted off to sleep. He dreamed of those white frosted fields of a winter long gone by. He dreamed of Solomon who for once was not hanging from a tree, but was standing with the girl he had become a turncoat for, smiling and Mullone could see how happy he looked. He was how he remembered him when he was alive, and Solomon hugged him, told him how much he loved him, and with that last embrace, he ran away to where shapes moved in the dream-fog. Solomon waved once more and Mullone opened his eyes.

He got up and blinked away the tears that had fallen to soak his shirt. He put on his boots and walked outside to check on the sentries. His timepiece showed it was just after four o'clock. It was quiet outside, and poisonous plumes of cloud continued to drift from New Ross. Down in the meadows was an old stone church, a ruin, and it looked like a jutting black rock amongst the tall grass. He took a lungful of breath, happy of the dream. He felt light, as though a burden was gone. Solomon had found peace. It was time that he did too.

The first blow struck his temple, and his vision exploded in showering stars. Mullone stumbled backwards against the house and hands grabbed his arms tightly. He made no attempt to draw his sword, knowing it would be futile. Another blow smacked the side of his head and Mullone knew nothing more.

A bucket of cold water splashed over his face and Mullone woke from his unconsciousness to a cold, bleary and pain-filled semi-darkness. Blood crusted his hair and had dripped down to stain his shirt underneath his open scarlet coat. He was on a chair and his hands were tied around his back.

Shadows took on weight and form. They watched him, and he could hear them whispering.

'Who are you after?' a voice said in Gaelic.

Mullone shook his head to clear his eyes, but that made the pain in his head even worse. The man asked him the same thing in English and when Mullone did not reply, a shadow stepped forward and a fist struck his face.

'Answer the question!' the man who had hit him bellowed.

More pain and more explosions of stars. 'In Gaelic?' Mullone asked, as water dripped from his chin.

'Answer the question!'

'Black,' Mullone said in Gaelic, tasting the salty tang of blood in his mouth. 'My orders are to find Colonel Black. We're not here for revenge, or to seize any one from the United Irishmen. I just want that bastard Black.' There was a silence in the room that caused a chill to go up his spine. 'Where are my men?'

No one answered.

'Where are they?' Mullone shouted.

'Dead,' said a voice in English and Mullone recognised it instantly.

There was a silence.

'Michael?'

McBride stepped forward. He was wearing civilian clothes and a green sash. 'Sir,' he said in acknowledgment. His eyes showed defiance but also a sense of sorrow.

'Dead?' Mullone couldn't believe it. 'Y-You let them be killed?' he said accusingly. He shook his arms, tearing at ropes around his hands and the man hit him again. 'You treacherous ‾ !' he shouted, his voice was thick from the springing blood in his mouth, and he had to spit to speak. 'You had them killed, Michael? Our boys? You had them murdered?'

'No, he did not,' a voice said. 'I did.' Another man, tall, blue-eyed and handsome, stepped forward.

'Why?' Mullone asked. Sweat prickled the back of his neck.

'They died because they were wearing the red coat and nothing more,' the man said matter-of-factly. 'Michael was the one that spared your life; otherwise, you'd have died in your sleep like your men.'

Mullone recognised him from New Ross. He had been the brave man who had rallied the attackers at Three Bullet Gate. He was wearing the green coat which was faced red, and decorated in gold lace. He wore a bright green sash and on his coat were two epaulettes of gold. His uniform was dazzling and immaculate compared to everyone else.

'My name is Fitzstephen,' the man continued. 'I'm sure you know who I am.'

'A United man,' Mullone replied.

Fitzstephen took several steps towards Mullone. 'We all are,' he said, gesturing at his men. 'And I know you and your dragoons were at New Ross. I had some trouble asking my men to stop from killing you too. You see they lost a good number of their friends and kin, but I know you're Moore's man and you've not come to stalk us revolutionaries.' He grinned widely when Mullone frowned at his knowledge. 'I knew that even before Michael joined us. I know a lot of things.' He bent closer to Mullone so that he could smell the blood. 'You see that we have acquaintances all over the country. In Belfast, Dublin and even in London. I even spoke with Lord Lovell in Parliament once. And of course we even have the same enemies.' Mullone knew who he meant. 'Colonel Black.' Fitzstephen dipped his head at the man to Mullone's right and the next thing Mullone felt his bonds cut. 'We're after the same man, Major, only for different reasons. Where were you heading?'

Mullone rubbed his wrists and asked for some water. A jug was fetched and brought to him. He drank to swill out saliva and blood. 'Enniscorthy,' he lied.

The rebels began to talk amongst themselves. Mullone could not believe his men were dead. He rubbed his battered face.

'You said that you were after Black?'

'I did,' Fitzstephen said.

'Would it have something to do with him hunting down men in the Wicklow Mountains?'

'How did you know that?'

'Colonel Moore told me that he had set them free from gaol, only to let his men charge them down.'

'One of them was a young cousin of mine and they were not charged with anything. They were locked up because a Militia captain picked them out of a crowd. My cousin was not even twelve years of age. Black simply slaughtered them,' Fitzstephen grew angrier until he took control of his feelings. 'You have been charged to bring him in to the authorities,' he said, then laughed scathingly. 'What are they going to do at the Castle? What punishment will he get? Where's the justice?'

'He will be tried publically in a court of law,' Mullone told him, knowing that it sounded weak.

'The man will get proper justice. The Irish way.' The hubbub of agreement echoed around the room. 'What do you know of a man called Sir Edward Clanfield?'

'I've heard of him,' Mullone answered. 'I don't know the man personally.'

'He rides with the devil,' said a large man stepping forth. 'We're going to expose him publically for his crimes against the Irish people.'

Mullone eyed him, noticing a familiarity in the man who had approached him in New Ross. 'Expose him for what?'

'The true man that he is.'

'Are you Scurlock?'

The man grunted. 'I am.'

'You escaped the slaughter at *Uaimh Tyrell*, but Colonel Black was tracking you. You then tried to find Fitzstephen in New Ross, but your luck ran out and you were caught.' He cast an eye over his young bespectacled officer. 'You broke Scurlock out of gaol, didn't you, Michael?'

'Aye, sir.'

Mullone rubbed his sore temple. His gaze rested on Scurlock. 'Your brother approached me and told me that you were going after Black.'

Scurlock shifted as though he was offended. 'My brother and I don't see eye-to-eye much these days. But the one thing we do agree about is the murder committed by both sides. Sir Edward, a man of noble birth, is as guilty as Black. He will be punished. Liberty or death!'

The gathered men chanted the axiom loudly.

A thought fluttered into Mullone's head. There were some rebels still in shadow. 'Where's De Marin?' The room went silent. 'I know who he is Fitzstephen. I am fully aware of your association with him. You're a supporter of Tone and Bonaparte, and De Marin is your wee French messenger. I knew that before Bantry Bay.' Now it was time for Fitzstephen to gawk in surprise. 'De Marin!' he shouted the name. 'Show yourself, you wretched devil!'

There was another stiff silence.

De Marin stepped out of the gloom.

'*Bonjour, mon ami,*' he said with a grin and an elegant bow. He was dressed in his priest's garb.

Mullone wanted nothing more than to reach for sword and stab this man through his conniving heart. He stared at the Frenchman who had eluded him for so long. Now, he reckoned his chances of leaving this barn were now nonexistent. De Marin would not let him live, but have him tortured for information first.

'You're a murdering bastard,' Mullone spat at his foe, whose lips twitched with amusement and he bowed again. 'You wear those robes as though God can protect you. Only He can know what you've done to stoke this country's rage. You've whispered and plotted and planned and deceived. Men, women and children have died. One day I'll see you dead.'

The Frenchman's lips pulled back from his teeth. 'I wouldn't bet on it now, *mon ami*.' He laughed. 'You're going to die.'

'Someone is,' Mullone shot him a malevolent look. 'Well, Mister Fitzstephen,' he mocked, 'what will you do now that you have me?'

'Run the bastard through where he sits,' suggested one of the rebels.

'Aye, death to the king's men!' another uttered.

The United leader listened to the remarks. He rubbed the stubble on his chin and looked at the major with thoughtful eyes. 'You are released,' he said with a wave, and Mullone was so startled with the reply that he did not move.

De Marin gaped like a village idiot. 'Surely you jest? *Non?* You can't let him go! He's working for the British government. He is a spy! He is worth a lot to me dead!' He burst into hurried French and Fitzstephen pushed him away with distaste.

'Moore sent him to find Black, so let him continue his wee quest to Enniscorthy. He is alone, his men are dead, and I have no use for him. He poses no threat. Go!' he said to Mullone.

Mullone rose as De Marin and Fitzstephen broke into a heated argument. He made for the door, a man handed him his sword belt. It was McBride.

'You are a good man, sir,' he said. 'I didn't want them to kill you. I just wanted you to know that.'

Mullone offered him a wounded look before turning to leave.

'All roads lead to the same direction, Major,' De Marin said as Mullone walked past. His eyes shone like two cruel gems. 'We shall meet again, *non?*'

Mullone wiped his lips of blood. 'Indeed we will, Father,' he said and then thumped the Frenchman hard in the stomach. De Marin doubled over in pain, writhing and gasping for air. 'God punishes false prophets,' Mullone spat.

Fitzstephen followed him outside.

'I truly hate that man,' Mullone said to no one in particular.

'Fetch the Major's horse,' Fitzstephen ordered one of his men. The man, wearing a captured Highlanders bonnet and a musket slung over his shoulder, disappeared momentarily before returning with

Tintreach, much to Mullone's utter delight. The United men had allowed Mullone to take his carbine and sword, as well as all his possessions with him. 'He's a fine stallion.'

'He is,' Mullone answered curtly, and grasped the reins tightly.

'Are you a patriot?' Fitzstephen asked him as he climbed up into his saddle. Mullone pushed his left boot into the stirrup, grimaced from the wound, and then lifted his body to flick out the tails of his scarlet coat. He clapped *Tintreach's* muscular neck and the beast snorted and bobbed its head with affection.

'I like to think so,' he said bitterly, because he could see naked legs and feet poking out from behind the barn. His men. Murdered in their beds, or where they stood and now dumped in a pile where flies feasted on the blood. He fought back a surge of tears.

'So am I, Major, but you wear the scarlet coat. Why is that if we are the same?'

Mullone let his gaze fall upon the rebel commander. 'I have worn this for more than thirty years. I wear it because I'd rather serve the British Crown as a free man, than be a slave to the French.'

Fitzstephen looked solemn.

Mullone glanced at the bodies again and his heart thumped in his chest, whilst theirs were growing cold. 'Give them a proper burial. It's what they deserve as Irishmen.'

He gave *Tintreach* his heels and rode north to warn Sir Edward.

Clanfield Manor was a spectacular sight. It was nestled above a small wood of pine and alder. A long gravel drive spiralled up from the road to Enniscorthy, and dotted with all manner of wild flowers. Outside the gates Mullone was stopped by a group of hard-looking men armed with swords and carbines. They let him pass by calling down a pleasant young man who introduced himself as Aengus, Sir Edward's major domo.

'Sir Edward sends his sincere apologies for the reception.' He saw the blood and bruises on Mullone's face. 'Are you in need of attention, Major? Shall I send for Dr Dalton?'

'No, I'm fine.' Mullone waved the empathy away. 'I've come from New Ross to warn Sir Edward of an attack.' Sunlight flashed on a pair of large rectangular windows overlooking the courtyard. He couldn't see anybody inside.

'My lord has received several death threats in the last forty-eight hours,' he said, gesturing to the guards, 'so we've placed men at the gates and we're taking every precaution as you can see.'

'Who are they?'

'They all work for Sir Edward,' Aengus shrugged as if there was no other way of answering the question. 'Things haven't been the same here since Sir Edward's brother died. Sir Charles. Poor man,' he sighed as though he found it too much to explain. 'A gang of rebels ambushed him and his servant on their way to Dublin. Both were robbed and murdered. A dreadful act of violence. The whole family are still in shock.'

'I was unaware of that. I shall pass on my condolences.'

'Thank you.'

A man with huge arms and thick lips led *Tintreach* to the stables while Aengus took him up several steps to the main entrance. Something was trying to get his attention, but Mullone was taken to the foyer where polished tiles gleamed, and then dully escorted to a room nearest the winding stairs. It was his lordship's private study.

Sir Edward was a handsome man, slim, dark-haired with a long sloping nose. He had none of the usual cold arrogance of the gentry and welcomed Mullone to his home as a friend and then shuddered at the bruises and dried blood. 'My dear fellow,' he said, 'what has happened to you?'

'I'll explain in due course, Sir Edward.'

'Then, please do have a seat.'

Mullone quickly eyed the many volumes with their rich covered bindings that adorned the shelves and tall cases. 'Thank you.'

'Now, what brings you here?'

'Firstly, please accept my condolences regarding your brother.'

'Thank you, Major,' Sir Edward said appreciatively.

'This conflict has seen the deaths of so many people. Any indication as to why he was targeted?'

'My brother was a staunch patriot and a loyal servant of the king.' Sir Edward suddenly looked as though he would wring Mullone's neck, but the major recognised the pain of losing kin and having to speak about it. 'That's why he was slain by craven murderers.' He blew out his cheeks. 'Charles was a good soul and his needless death in these volatile times has shattered my family. My eldest sister has miscarried and my ailing mother now confines herself to her house due to depression and fear. I loved my brother as any man could. Poor Charles was set upon like hounds taking down a fox. He never stood a chance. Now, why have you come to see me?'

'I believe that your life is in danger.'

Sir Edward did something that Mullone certainly did not expect. He laughed.

'My dear fellow, since this insurrection broke out I've had death threats nearly every week. I've had the odd tenant come to me with his complaints, and I've even had one threaten me with a hammer, but I take it in my stride as their landlord. I have come to expect it.'

'It's no laughing matter, sir,' Mullone said. 'I have first-hand accounts to say the rebels are coming here in force.'

'How could you possibly know this?'

'Because my men and I were stabled a wee way from here and a group of rebels murdered them all in their beds. We had just left the devastation of New Ross. They questioned me and let me go when I told them I was going to Enniscorthy, but I've come here to warn you instead.'

Sir Edward looked pained. 'My God! They couldn't have picked a better night for it. Most of the men working for me have returned to their homes. I have my wife, my three oldest friends and their wives staying with us. They are in the dining room right as I speak. I shall ask them to leave immediately.'

'Very good, and summon your guards, sir,' Mullone said. 'I need to talk to them first.'

Sir Edward shot him an inquisitive look. 'What for?'

'To make sure they're willing to fight.'

Sir Edward opened one of the drawers of a desk and bundled something into a pocket. They then hurried to the dining room, boots thumped loudly on the wooden floors down two long corridors to the back of the house. Sir Edward flung open the large door, startling a man examining the silver cutlery. He was dressed in the finery of an aristocrat: a plain dark-blue coat, tight-fitting and cut away, forming curving tails. His waistcoat of the same colour was shortened to just below the waist and his cream-coloured breeches were worn tight. It would have been fashionable to wear a powdered wig, dressed high and tied at the back, but there had been a recent tax imposed on hair powder by William Pitt, and the landed gentry had promptly abandoned them.

Sir Edward opened his mouth, when there was a shout outside in the gardens, followed by a musket shot.

'What's going on, Eddie?' asked the man.

'Troublemakers, Iollan,' Sir Edward replied calmly. 'Nothing for you to concern yourself with. Take some more claret.'

Iollan gazed at Mullone, grimacing at the bruises and cuts. 'If there's nothing to worry about, then what's he doing here?'

One of the female guests gasped and Sir Edward went to the large double doors and for a moment he could see nothing on the cut lawn, but then in the shadows of the hedgerows, he saw the glint of metal and a cold sensation went up his spine as several unfamiliar faces stared straight back at him.

'Get back, sir!' a hand seized and pulled him back as a musket flashed and the bullet struck to shatter the window where Sir Edward had been standing. Mullone had seen the movement and had known immediately what would happen. Lady Ellen Clanfield screamed and one of the guests whimpered.

'The house is under-siege, Sir Edward!' Mullone told him hurriedly. 'Are the front doors locked?'

'No, I don't think so.'

'What about your men, Eddie?' asked Iollan, his voice distant as though he was struggling to comprehend the implication of being attacked. 'They were posted at the gates.'

'They're out there still,' said Sir Edward.

'A handful might still be alive, but the rest will be dead, or most likely gone over to the enemy,' Mullone said dismissively.

Iollan went wide-eyed. 'What?'

A man with a white shirt, brown breeches and a white neck-tie stood up. 'Are we under attack?'

Iollan shook his head in frustration. 'Yes, Bartley!'

Bartley tottered a few steps before crossing himself.

'My men are loyal to me, Major,' Sir Edward vehemently. 'They will fight for me!'

'Let's hope they can, Eddie,' said the other male guest. He was dressed in a white frilly shirt. He had a shock of fiery-red hair and seemed to be trembling. He emptied a wineglass and poured himself another drink, spilling wine over the tablecloth.

Mullone edged beside a window, but could see nothing outside. 'If they still live,' he said, matter-of-factly.

'Oh, Edward!' Lady Ellen cried.

Sir Edward strode over to her, arms grasping hers. 'There, there, my sweet. Calm yourself. Everything will be fine. Just some warmongers outside, trying to intimidate us with violence. I told you they would try something like this. But I have taken safety measures.'

'They're going to kill us, Edward,' she replied, tears threatening to spoil her cornflower blue dress.

'Nonsense, my sweet.'

Another musket banged and a man screamed. He began to gasp for breath; each exhalation a terrible, pitiful moan. Then, he went quiet.

'Are the doors locked?' Mullone didn't wait for Sir Edward to answer and went over to the door that led to the rest of the house. He opened it slowly and it creaked. He moved quietly down the semi-darkened corridor; his heart beating fast in his chest, but could see or hear no indication of a break-in. He wished he had remembered to unsheathe his carbine, but *Tintreach* and his other equipment were in the stables. Then, there was a thud and floorboards creaked somewhere down in the near hallway. Mullone instinctively sensed danger and flung himself aside as a pistol flamed brightly in the shadows.

A voice shouted behind him. 'Show yourself, you lowborn villains!'

'Get back inside!' Mullone snarled as Bartley had ventured into the corridor. One of the household had appeared from the kitchen with two hunting rifles and a flask of powder and shot. It was Aengus. 'Inside! All of you! Now!'

He pushed the men forcefully into the room as another bullet smacked into the lintel above his head. Voices cursed him. The door slammed behind and a large sideboard was dragged across the floor to reinforce the door.

'I hope that's enough,' Mullone said.

'Liam, stoke the fire,' Sir Edward told one of the servants. He turned to Mullone. 'I've bullet moulds and lead bars should we need to make more shot.'

'Good thinking, sir.'

'Liam, load the blunderbuss too,' Sir Edward said, taking the cumbersome weapon from its wall mountings. He turned to the women. 'Ladies, please remove yourself from the vicinity and relocate at the rear wall. My dear, Ellen, that means you too. Keevan, would you escort my wife?' The red-haired man nodded emphatically. 'Ladies, please find appropriate cover: chairs, the display cabinet . . .'

Suddenly, the door thudded and one of the women whimpered. Bartley took an old sword hanging above the fireplace, marched to the door and swore at the intruders. A bullet tore through the wood, making him jump aside. Aengus fired one of the two hunting rifles through the large paned window and was rewarded with a yelp. He passed the unloaded rifle to the servant known as Liam. A musket shot splintered a pane and the glass crashed on the floor. Mullone helped tip the large dining table over, plates, cups, glasses, bowls and cutlery clattered and smashed onto the floor. Mullone, Sir Edward, Keevan and Iollan dragged the table against the window. Bullets crashed through the glass to make holes in the wood. Shadows blurred outside and Mullone withdrew his sword.

'Watch out!' he snarled as a man wearing a green sash smashed the glass and a pike sliced into the opening. Mullone hammered the weapon away before it thrust up into Sir Edward's neck.

'Thank you, Major,' Sir Edward said graciously.

A blast of musketry shattered more glass and the women screamed. An oil painting showing an ancestor from the 17th century was shot through and collapsed in a broken heap onto the floor. An axe thudded into the table and hands clawed at the wood from outside. Mullone slapped them away and kicked at fingers.

'We'll burn your house down, you devil!' a voice shouted from outside.

'God damn the king's men!' said another.

'Give me a weapon, for God's sake!' begged Iollan.

Sir Edward reached into a coat pocket and tossed him a pistol. The guest caught it. 'It's loaded, so save your shot!'

Aengus brought up a rifle, aiming at a shadow and pulled the trigger. The gun rammed into his shoulder and blotted his view with smoke. The third servant was armed with a carbine and tracked a shape outside in the green chaos and pulled the trigger. He didn't wait to see if he had hit anything, he simply began to load. The air was hissing with bullets, endless with the noise of muskets firing and the dull rattle of ramrods.

'There's one!' Iollan shouted, aimed his pistol and wasted the shot because he'd fired too soon. Gun smoke was wafting over their heads to touch the high ceiling like patchy grey clouds.

A bullet whipped close to Mullone, tearing at a silver epaulette. The gun smoke was getting thicker now, and he strained to see the grounds outside.

A carbine cracked and Aengus was shot in the neck. The force knocked him backwards, astonishment on his face, and blood spraying over Liam. He tried to speak, but blood spilled from his slack mouth.

Sir Edward's eyes bored into Liam's for an answer and the servant shook his head gravely. 'You murdering knaves!' the aristocrat raged at the attackers.

The door shook. Hands and boots banged and thumped it. Then, an axe head smashed through the wood and a muzzle appeared.

'You cowardly wretches!' Bartley shouted and the gun flashed to send him sprawling.

The door trembled as men shouldered and kicked at it. The sideboard slid across the floor.

'Here they come!' Mullone bellowed, bringing his sword to bear.

The door burst open. Three men wearing green cockades in their hats stood at the doorway, momentarily confused at the new surroundings and in that pause Sir Edward grabbed the blunderbuss from the footman and pulled the trigger. The gun went off like a small cannon, its noise deafening the room, and the rebels were snatched off their feet by the charge. Blood and gore splattered the door and wall behind. One of the traumatised women was screaming incoherently until she was slapped across the face into silence by another.

No enemies entered the room as the sound of the gun faded away. Mullone took tentative steps towards the door, his boots crunched over shattered glass, plaster, broken chinaware and cartridge wadding. There was an eerie silence, punctuated by Sir Edward asking if everyone was all right. Mullone's pulse settled because no enemies charged, no priming pans flared and no pikes sliced at him.

'Stay where you are, Major,' a deep voice boomed from the doorway.

Mullone stopped instantly. 'We have women in here,' he said. 'Let's put away the weapons. There's been enough bloodshed. Let us talk.'

A big man stepped through the gun smoke and Mullone saw that he was unarmed. It was Scurlock. He wore his long grey coat and his white shirt underneath was blood-stained signifying that he had been wounded in the attack.

'There's nothing left to say,' he said grimly, 'but I will show you the devil.'

Something clicked behind and Mullone spun round.

'No!' he yelled, but the doghead snapped forward, the flint sparked and the pistol flared. The bullet drummed into Scurlock's chest and he fell backward, wide-eyed against the wall. Mullone turned, bent down to him, but the smith was already dead.

Sir Edward lowered the pistol and gasped an intake of breath. 'Dear God, is it over? Have they gone?'

The rebels did not attack the house again.

Sir Edward ventured out into the rest of the house with a handful of servants who had survived the attack in the gardens. The enemy had gone, patches of smoke still wisped and the dead were slumped like string-cut puppets. He thanked Mullone by pumping his hand energetically and promised that he would write a report and send it to the viceroy gratefully acknowledging his service and heroism.

'Thank you, sir,' Mullone said jadedly, his resolve dampened by the attack.

'Where are you headed now?'

Mullone looked distant. 'New Ross, sir,' he said. 'To see a friend.'

*

Two days passed by.

Sir Edward, dressed in a sober black coat, plain shirt and snow-white breeches, opened the front door of his house, the lantern's light casting flickering shadows. There were no servants left, they had been sent to Dublin with Ellen, and the manor was left dark, silent and bare. The doors and stonework were pockmarked by musket fire and scarred from axe, pike and sword blows. He entered through the heavy doors with a lantern, confident that no harm would befall him. He had sent out two of his footmen to New Ross to determine the siege to find that the rebels had failed and hundreds were said to have been slain. The town was in loyalist hands and it seemed that the attack on his house was also a crippling blow to them. The rebels had destroyed many of his ornaments and stolen a lot more, but he was grateful to have survived the attack along with his doting wife. The remaining servants had hurriedly loaded as much of their possessions onto the four coaches for the journey to Dublin, but there were a few things left for him to collect and take care of.

Sir Edward made his way to the dining room that had witnessed so much destruction that night. The floor had been scrubbed of blood, but there were still dark stains where men had died. His old friend Bartley had taken a bullet to the lung and there was nothing that anyone could do to save him. His major domo, Aengus McGifford, had died instantly.

He walked down to the study and put the lamp on his writing desk and gathered some paperwork from inside a drawer. He saw that his pistol, one of two, was still there when a noise from behind him made the hairs on the back of his neck stand on end. His hand went for the pistol, but a voice spoke and he went utterly still.

'I still never understood why the rebels came for you that night when there was an artillery train ripe for plundering on the Wexford road.'

Sir Edward did not recognise the voice at first until Mullone moved out of shadow. 'Major, my dear chap,' he sighed exasperatedly. 'What are you doing there in the dark? I presumed you were in New Ross?'

'I was just thinking how lucky we were that night when the mob came,' Mullone said distantly.

Sir Edward stared down at the major's half-shadowed body, his eyes were like white orbs in the light. He was sitting on one of the green chairs that belonged to Ellen's grandfather. He straightened and turned fully so that he faced Mullone.

'Quite so. I thank God for it. I owe you my life, dear friend. We all do,' he said, smiling. 'I'm about to finish that report. Do you want to see a copy of it?'

'Not now, your Lordship,' Mullone said calmly.

'Would you like a drink?'

'Yes,' Mullone rasped, 'more than anything in the world, but I'd better not.'

Sir Edward brought out a bottle of whiskey and a small tumbler emblazoned with his family's crest.

'I was sent from the Castle by Colonel John Moore on a wee errand. Do you know what it was? I'll tell you,' he said when the peer shrugged. 'It was to find the man responsible for the atrocity committed at *Uaimh Tyrell*. A poor fishing village of not much else. A few families lived there.'

'Yes, I've heard of it. It was in all the papers.'

'A horrific crime was committed there.'

'So I read.'

'There were no survivors, and yet, there was a rumour that Colonel Black was responsible.'

Sir Edward chuckled, shaking his head. 'That creature? A crime is committed from petty thievery to murder and the peasants blame it on Black. He doesn't actually exist, you know. It's a rumour made up by the press to sell their damned stories.'

'Oh, but that's where I think you're wrong. He does exist, Sir Edward,' Mullone said. 'He's as real as rainfall and sunshine. It was said that the people of *Uaimh Tyrell* were good Protestants and good Catholics. They certainly weren't slaughtered by rumour.'

Sir Edward seemed to shudder as though his shoulders had been hit with a cudgel. 'A heinous crime.'

'They had nothing to do with the rebellion. They were not hiding fugitives.'

'So the priest said,' Sir Edward replied, taking a large gulp of the whiskey.

'Perhaps he really didn't know.'

'Priests are the eyes of the rebels, Major. He knew. He was just being stubborn.'

Mullone stared.

'And how would you know that, your Lordship?' he said after a moment of silence.

Sir Edward said nothing as though he was replaying the last sentence in his head. He blinked, then brought out the pistol. He opened the frizzen and checked that the flint was in place. He brought the doghead back until it clicked. The sound was loud in the small darkened room.

'It's a beautiful instrument,' Mullone said.

'Yes,' the aristocrat replied, long fingers stroking the barrel.

'It must have cost a lot of money.'

'It's one of a pair. Rifled with absolute precision and made by a craftsman in Germany called Lang. Cost a fortune, but they're worth every pound.'

Mullone remained seated; he watched the pistol in Sir Edward's hands where he jiggled it from one to the other.

'It struck me that your footmen knew how to load firearms,' Mullone said.

'I prefer that they do. A score of them accompany me during the hunting season. Armed retainers are what keep this manor safe. Other owners have failed to understand that and have now paid with their lives.'

'One of your guards was even wearing regulation white breeches. Cavalry breeches. They screamed at me when I arrived here, but I was too preoccupied with trying to warn you. Ever been to Oldbridge?'

The nobleman did not reply. He appeared to be occupied by the silver design on the pistol's grip that were full of hunting scenes: horses, hounds and a fox.

Mullone rubbed an eye, as though he was tired. 'What happened to your brother?'

'I told you. He was murdered,' Sir Edward's voice was suddenly cold. 'What has that got to do with your errand?'

'Was he killed chasing rebels?' Mullone asked. 'He died at Oldbridge, didn't he? That fellow Scurlock was the one you were after. He had something to do with your brother's death and you tracked him all the way to *Uaimh Tyrell*. But he wasn't there, was he? No matter. The people there knew him by association so they had to die too. Isn't that right? But what about the others you've killed along the way in your quest for retribution? What about the prisoners you hunted down in Wicklow? The family the press say were nailed to the doors because it was said they once let Scurlock sleep in their barn. Was it a game to you? A blood sport?'

Sir Edward chuckled in wry amusement. 'You don't know what you are talking about, Major. You're babbling. I fear the tragic events of New Ross have disturbed your mind.'

'I've never felt so alive, or thought so clearly, Sir Edward,' Mullone said. 'Or do you prefer being called Colonel Black?' The aristocrat said nothing and stared back at the pistol, turning it as though it was a rare gem. 'But it wasn't your brother's death that spurned you on your vile task, was it? You were hunting and murdering people long before that. You were Black long before the news of *Uaimh Tyrell* spread from one village to another until the country knew the crime. But now Scurlock is dead and your quest is over. I am under orders to bring you to Dublin where you will be tried.'

Sir Edward laughed again; the noise sounding like a snort. 'And what makes you so certain that I would willingly agree?' He raised the pistol to Mullone's face.

Mullone seemed unfazed by the threat. 'So we meet at last, Colonel Black,' he breathed.

Sir Edward gazed at him with mock surprise. 'And when did you become so wise?' he said, mockingly.

'It is not wisdom, Sir Edward; it is truth. The path to fact is always clear, if you look straight at it. I wasn't looking clearly enough, but I am now.'

'The path you tread will get you killed, Major. I will not confess. I am no one's puppet!' A smile nestled on Sir Edward's handsome face as he pulled the trigger.

And to his absolute horror, nothing happened.

'I thought you'd say that,' Mullone said with a long sigh. 'So I took the liberty of swapping your pistol with its twin. You said it was one of a pair, and I knew where you'd keep it.' Mullone brought the second pistol up to Sir Edward's face. 'They are marvellous,' he conceded. 'There's a harsh beauty about them.'

The aristocrat looked outraged, then smiled like the cold embrace of winter. 'You won't do it. I'm too valuable alive. You will have to prove your accusations and I'll have the best lawyers defending me. English ones. I'll see you cashiered. Ruined. Your career left in tatters. No one will find out the truth.' He gazed at the door and then at the window that would spill glorious early morning light onto the desk, illuminating the parchments with a rich glow. Now, darkness cloaked the grounds outside.

'You wouldn't be expecting Seamus, now would you, Sir Edward?' Mullone asked innocently.

Sir Edward's defiant face cracked. 'He...' his voice trailed off.

'He was a bullock of a man! And he was a surprisingly good talker too, but then he wanted to murder me, so I spilled his guts on your neat lawn. He was easy to spot in his uniform.'

Sir Edward eyed the weapon's black mouth, his jaw clenched. 'You're not a murderer. You won't do it.'

'Oh, I will, Sir Edward,' Mullone said softly, 'and I hate you for making me do it.'

The shot echoed from the house and pounded across the fields.

*

The clock in the room struck twelve of the morning. It was July 1st.

Colonel John Moore eyeballed the man who had just walked into the room at Wexford and delivered news that stunned the Scotsman into silence.

'Are you telling me that you didn't find Black?' Moore said when the chimes had died and he had found his voice.

'Yes, sir,' Mullone said, looking up from his report on the desk.

Moore's eyes flicked left to right, taking in every detail of Mullone's green eyes, like hooks snagging flesh. 'Do you have any leads? Anything at all?'

'No, sir. In the week since the Battle of Vinegar Hill I've not been able to trace his whereabouts. It's as if the ground has swallowed him up.'

On the 21st June, British forces launched an attack on Vinegar Hill outside the town of Enniscorthy, hoping to encircle and destroy the large rebel camp there. It was a brutal battle that spilled down into the streets.

'Then Black is still at large and we have failed,' Moore stated, giving Mullone a look of despair, before staring at the report again.

Mullone said nothing. A bat flew past the window, fluttering in the moonlight before disappearing. The deep waters of the River Slaney seemed to shiver.

'You came recommended,' Moore said with a glare, not hiding the severe disappointment that was affecting him, 'highly recommended. I am surprised. I presumed you would detain him. There really are no leads?'

'No, sir.'

'You make it clear in your report that De Marin was one of the ringleaders.'

'Yes, sir. He was at Enniscorthy on the 21st, but alas, he got away when the rebels blockaded the bridge preventing General Johnson's advance. I'm sure we'll meet again.'

'Have you the same confidence about Black?' Moore said bluntly, then rubbed his tired eyes. 'I understand about men slinking off into the shadows.' A day before Vinegar Hill, Colonel Moore, with orders from the Castle, had encountered a rebel force on the road to Wexford and defeated them as the shadowy ambushers struck from the hills, woods and fields. The army survived and the rebels melded away. 'I understand you and your men helped defend New Ross against Fitzstephen's rebels. General Johnson's report is most satisfactory.'

'Thank you, sir.'

'I'm sorry to hear about the loss of your men. I understand that your sergeant was wounded during the assault and your lieutenant was killed in the fighting.'

Mullone cleared his throat. 'Yes, sir,' he said, feeling uneasy about the lie.

Cahill was recuperating and Michael had chosen his true allegiance. He felt for the boy, had mentored him and he honestly hoped McBride would one day find reconciliation.

Moore pulled a letter to him. 'Do you know that they found Sir Edward Clanfield dead?'

'No, sir.'

'You aren't shocked?'

'I didn't really know him,' Mullone replied innocuously.

'His manor was attacked twice by insurgents. It seems they came back sometime later after the first assault and finished the job. Probably by a group eager for plunder and destruction following their defeat at New Ross.'

'We live in sad times, sir.'

'His poor wife is related to the Under-Secretary. Tragic.' Moore put the letter down and sighed. 'You've no doubt heard about the boats docked at Brest and Toulon?'

'Bonaparte's invasion fleet.'

'Which we now know is not bound for England, or these shores. You have your orders with you?'

'I do, sir,' Mullone replied. Government papers, for his eyes only.

'Well, God speed in your new adventure,' Moore stood up and clasped his hand, sighing. 'I just wish we'd got him,' he was still gripping the Irishman's hand.

'I know, sir,' Mullone replied humbly.

'If there's a shred of something good to come out of this tragedy, I wanted him stopped. He's been absent of late, but maybe we'll get him next time. I truly hope so.' Moore relaxed and withdrew his arm. 'Goodbye, Lorn.'

'Goodbye, sir.'

Mullone left the room for his quarters. He would only have a four hours' sleep, because at dawn he was expected to be at the harbour where he was to join a ship bound for London.

General Bonaparte and the French fleet were rumoured to be sailing for India to ally themselves with the ruler of Mysore to help destroy Britain's trade, but this was another fabrication.

Mullone fingered the cross at his neck and before going to bed, he said his prayers; for his friends and for God to forgive him for his sins. He was going to a faraway place, away from friends, and he did not want to go. Ireland was still suffering and he had desperately wanted to stay, but an old enemy threatened, and so he had go where he was ordered to.

Mullone slept peacefully, and that night he dreamed of wind-blown temples, sun-scorched deserts, strange animals and a land as distant and exotic as any on God's beautiful earth.

Egypt.

HISTORICAL NOTE

The rebellion of 1798 was an uprising against British rule in Ireland lasting from May to September. Ultimately, it failed.

The Society of United Irishmen, a republican revolutionary group founded in Belfast, 1791, and influenced by the ideas of the American and French revolutions, were the main organising force behind it. They came together to secure a reform of the Irish parliament and did this by uniting Roman Catholics, Presbyterians, Methodists, other Protestant "dissenters" groups.

From the very beginning, Dublin Castle, the seat of government in Ireland, viewed the new organisation with suspicion, and with the outbreak of war between Britain (including Ireland) and France in February 1793, mistrust turned to naked hostility. The Society members were viewed as traitors and it was suppressed in 1794. Led by Theobald Wolf Tone, a barrister, he vowed to "break the connection with England" as the group was driven underground. A planned uprising with French military help resulted in a series of blunders and the first invasion faltered and the fleet sailed home.

The government responded to widespread disorders by launching a counter-campaign of martial law in early 1798. Its doctrines used tactics such as planting spies, half-hangings, house burnings, pitch-capping and murder, particularly found in Ulster as it was the one area of Ireland where Catholics and Protestants had achieved a common cause of revolt. A plan to take Dublin was thwarted, but just after sunrise on 24th May, pockets of insurgents rose and the fighting quickly spread throughout the country over the next four months.

The aftermath was marked by the massacres of captured and wounded rebels with some on a large scale such as at New Ross and

Enniscorthy. Rebel prisoners were regarded as traitors to the Crown, and were not treated as prisoners of war, but were executed. County Wexford was the only area which saw widespread atrocities committed by the rebels during the rebellion. Massacres of loyalist prisoners took place at the Vinegar Hill camp and on Wexford Bridge. After the defeat of the rebel attack at New Ross, the 'Scullabogue Barn Massacre' occurred where between one hundred and two hundred mostly Protestant men, women, and children were imprisoned in a barn which was then torched. In Wexford town, on 20th June some seventy loyalist prisoners were marched to the bridge and piked to death.

On 22nd August, one thousand French soldiers under General Humbert landed in County Mayo. Joined by several thousand rebels, they inflicted a humiliating defeat on the British at the Castlebar, which became mockingly known as the 'Castlebar races' to commemorate the speed of the retreat. But luck ran out for the French who were defeated and repatriated to France in exchange for British prisoners of war. For the hundreds of captured Irish rebels, their fate was the hangman's noose or firing squad.

On 12th October, another French force, including Wolfe Tone, attempted to land in County Donegal near Lough Swilly. They were intercepted by the Royal Navy, and finally surrendered after a three hour battle without ever landing in Ireland. Tone slit his own throat rather than wait for the noose and died a week later.

Small fragments of the rebel armies survived for a number of years and waged a form of guerrilla warfare in several counties. It was not until the failure of Robert Emmet's rebellion of 1803 that the last organised rebel force finally capitulated.

The Act of Union, having been passed in August 1800, came into effect on 1st January 1801. It was passed largely in response to the rebellion and was founded by the perception that the rebellion was provoked by the brutish misrule of the Ascendancy as much as the efforts of the United Irishmen.

The rebellion caused thousands of deaths. Modern accounts estimate the death toll from ten to as many as fifty thousand men, women and children killed by battle, starvation and disease.

Liberty or Death is a work of fiction, but firmly rooted by actual events. Lorn Mullone, Sergeant Cahill and the rebel leader John Fitzstephen are inventions, but men like Colonel John Moore, Colonel Robert Craufurd, General Henry Johnson and the pious Luke Gardiner, Colonel Lord Mountjoy, did exist. Lord Maxwell Lovell's Irish Dragoon regiment is another invention but based on the number of Yeomanry and Fencible regiments created at this time.

All of the locations mentioned are real except *Uaimh Tyrell*. The Battle of New Ross (actually the Second Battle of New Ross) did happen as much described. The rebels, under the leadership of Bagenal Harvey and John Kelly, tried to break out of County Wexford across the River Barrow to spread the rebellion into County Kilkenny and the outlying province of Munster. New Ross guarded the borders. The town was first fought over during the Irish Confederate Wars and captured by Cromwellian troops in 1649. Artillery fired three shots at the east gate and it was subsequently known thereafter as Three Bullet Gate.

The huge numbers of the rebel army swept aside the small military outposts and seized the gate. They then attacked simultaneously down the steeply sloping streets but were met with barricades and musket-armed soldiers. Despite a terrible number of casualties taken, the rebels managed to seize two-thirds of the town by using the cover of smoke from the burning buildings. Nonetheless, their limited supply of gunpowder and ammunition forced them to rely on the pike and that was no real match against well-trained volley fire. The soldiers under Johnson managed to hold on and following the arrival of reinforcements, launched a counterattack which finally drove the exhausted rebels away. The slaughter, plundering and destruction mentioned in the story are based on true eye-witness accounts. Rebel casualties have been reported at three thousand whilst Crown forces suffered about two hundred. Most of the rebel dead were either thrown in the Barrow, or buried in a mass grave outside the town walls in the aftermath.

By the nineteenth century New Ross had become a wealthy port, but thousands left to start new lives abroad. The most famous emigrants were the great-grandparents of John F. Kennedy, who visited his ancestral home in 1963.

Colonel Black is another creation, but derived from a group of looters who styled themselves 'The Black Mob' after the conflict coupled with the fear and murderous hatred that had sparked across the country. De Marin was invented as Mullone's nemesis; they have a history and will undoubtedly meet again as the Frenchman mockingly hopes.

For more information on the events of 1798, I recommend a visit to the Wexford Museum, which is very educational. I would also recommend reading Thomas Pakenham's *The Year of Liberty*, a masterly telling of that violent and deeply unfortunate chapter of Irish history.

David Cook
April, 2014
Hampshire

If you'd like to connect you can find me here at:

@davidcookauthor
www.facebook.com/davidcookauthor
http://davidcookauthor.blogspot.co.uk/
http://thewolfshead.tumblr.com

Printed in Great Britain
by Amazon

46172795R00068